My
Life
Outback

Arthur Upfield

ETT IMPRINT

Exile Bay

Publisher's Dedication
For Philip Austin
who with his father, helped create the BONEY Television series

First published into Imprint Classics by ETT Imprint in 2025

Copyright Williiam Upfield 2013, 2025

Transcribed and introduced by Tom Thompson

ETT IMPRINT
PO Box R1906
Royal Exchange NSW 1225 Australia

ISBN 9781923205932 (First edition - 50 Hardbacks)
ISBN 9781923205956 (Paperback)
ISBN 9781923205963 (Ebook)

Design by Tom Thompson

Contents

Introduction

Tom Thompson

In 1932 Arthur Upfield got a part-time job as a writer on the Melbourne *Herald*, courtesy of the great public interest in the case of "Snowy" Rowles, who murdered three men using ideas discussed within the then-unpublished Upfield 'Bony' thriller *The Sands of Windee*.

In September 1933, Arthur Upfield took up a six month contract writing for the Melbourne *Herald*, very determined to try and write for a living instead of working the land. He received only 5 guineas a week, with £2.10s going to his wife, which left him £2.15s to live on. He was still paying off the £14 owing on back rent of the Kalamunda house they'd rented, and a loan from J.K. Ewers at £1 pound a week. He tried to supplement this meagre salary by submitting literary stories outside the *Herald*.

The editor at the *Herald,* Sidney Deamer, commissioned him to write "a racing serial" - 'The Great Melbourne Cup Mystery' - in September over eight weeks, with Upfield even buying and selling a racehorse to get the gist of the track. The serial began in the Melbourne *Herald* on October 21 and in the *Adelaide Advertiser* (November 20 to December 14 1934).

It was successful enough that "Mr. Laby, the editor of *Sporting Globe*, thought the story would turn out all right, and he suggested that Upfield write a boxing serial for him."[1] Upfield had offered the final larger manuscript to Angus & Robertson who turned it down on 24 January 1934. They requested it again but Upfield had sent it to Peter J. O'Connell, his agent in England. While interest in Upfield's 'Bony' books accelerated, *The Great Melbourne Cup Mystery* would not be published until 1996.[2]

In December 1933 he wrote his friend from Perth, the author J.K (Keith) Ewers:[3]

"Next Wednesday I am going to live on the top of Mt Dandenong for two months. Two thousand feet above the sea and a sixty mile view from the front windows of the three room cottage I have taken at a pound per week. It is only an hour's run from the city and to me with my love of spaces a veritable paradise."

In 1934 Upfield convinced the *Herald* to advance him the money for fares for his wife and son James to come to Mt Dandenong.

In his time at the *Herald* he was encouraged by "Mr. Ralph Simmonds, then assistant editor, and next he wrote special articles for the magazine section and for column four of the leading article page. He wrote of the aboriginal problems, and of the neglected opportunities of development of the interior, and when he came up with a series of articles on outback adventures,[3] this series was announced on the contents bills and on the delivery vans. It was so successful that it was followed by a second series..."[4]

In February 1934 Upfield wrote to Ewers about the amount of work he had accomplished for the *Herald* the previous five months:

"Provided they accept the new *Breakaway*[5] - which I think is good - which will be finished on the 25th of the month, I shall have produced for the *Herald* 202,000 published words, or 10,000 words a week.

"I wrote for them a series of 12 biographical articles which they syndicated in four other papers. I was asked to produce a second series which I submitted yesterday. The wordage works out thus over the 5 months:

Cup Mystery   50,000
Breakaway   84,000
1st series of articles 24,000
2nd ditto 18,000
Special leader page and mag. article 16,400
Do you think this is good?...

"Despite all this I may be put on tramp next week. There is no security for anyone even the editors..."

The 12 autobiographical articles under the title 'My Life Outback' are now printed here as a group for the first time, and these were his initial attempt at an autobiography which he titled *The Tale of a Pommy*.[6]

Upfield's letter to Ewers was prescient - Upfield and 16 other writers were laid off from the *Herald* in March 1934, two weeks after he completed his six month contract. He wrote to Ewers on March 28th that his wife Anne had £2, he had £6 owing him, and that the *Herald* had agreed to cut him in on the second series of bush articles, 'The Real Australia', which would bring in a further £17.10s. Upfield was bitter with his life in such penury.

In a letter to Ewers dated July 17 1934, he noted his earnings were about £4 a week on the average. He also mentioned that two months before, he had written "a 15,000 word synopsis chapter by chapter of a Bony yarn concerning a derelict aeroplane *a la* Marie Celeste giving the job an Air Race background."[7] In the same letter he brings up some family news, writing that influenza had struck the family and that his son, James, had found a good teacher and was doing well in school moving from 5th to 8th Grade.

Things picked up a little by September. He wrote to Ewers on September 14: "I have been working on jobs for a new magazine to be brought out by the Australian Travel Association, as well as other stuff. I am happy to tell you that I can definitely see my way round a long and ugly corner, and that in the near future I hope to repay your loan."

That new magazine was *Walkabout* and Upfield's article, "Coming Down With Cattle", which describes a 700-mile cattle drive from southwestern Queensland to a railhead in South Australia, was the lead article in the first issue dated November 1st 1934. That was the start of a long association with *Walkabout* for which he wrote many articles over the years.[8]

Things were looking up. Upfield wrote to Ewers on November 18 from Mt Dandenong regarding a biography[9] he had been commissioned to write:

"I am just about to write the biography - from a typed MS poorly done - of a wealthy squatter living in South Yarra. I have given myself six months to do it, and am to be paid at the rate of £50 a month. His life is extraordinarily interesting. Came out here in '59, then went among the cannibals of the New Hebrides; and finally went to the far north of Queensland where he took up land and eventually sold it for £60,000, then bought and sold stations, and finally settled down and had racehorses for the fun of it."

Upfield's own costs to complete the biography of Frank Cobbold were higher than he first imaged, despite getting a free four-week chauffeur-driven tour of Cobbold's Queensland cattle stations in December 1934.

Upfield's time at the Melbourne *Herald* had given him hope and impetus, and the serialisation enforced a better understanding of how he could schedule the chapter and content of his future novels. His articles for *Walkabout* and the *Bulletin* finally got him through a most difficult year, a year crowned with the publication of his own account of the "Snowy" Rowles case, *The Murchison Murders*[9] - proving he could survive on his writing alone.

1. *Follow My Dust,* by Jessica Hawke with Arthur Upfield was first published in 1957. (ETT Imprint, 2015)

2. *The Great Melbourne Cup Mystery* (ETT Imprint, 1996)

3. All letters from J.K. Ewers are in the possession of Patricia Kotai-Ewers

4. *Follow My Dust,* as above.

5. Breakway - *Breakaway House* - was serialised in the Perth *Daily News* from September 1932, and ETT Imprint published this edition in 2015. Upfield began a rewrite of this for the *Herald,* who did not take it, and these five chapters are in *Up & Down Australia Again* (ETT Imprint 2017)

6. *The Tale of a Pommy,* (University of Melbourne, Baillieu Library, Sp/C). This manuscript finally became *Beyond the Mirage* completed in 1938, but not published until 2020 by ETT Imprint

7. Upfield's first stab at what became the third Bony novel - *Wings Above the Diamantina,* first published in 1937 (ETT Imprint, 2020)

8. Upfield's entire output for the magazine was published as *Walkabout* (ETT Imprint, 2021)

9. *The Gifts of Frank Cobbold* was intended to be published by Cobbold in England in 1935, but finally available from ETT Imprint in 2015

10. *The Murchison Murders* was rejected by Hutchinson in London in 1932 and by Angus & Robertson in 1933. It was published by The Midget Masterpiece Publishing Company in Sydney, and is now an Imprint Classic in 2025

Arthur Upfield
in 1911.

Arthur Upfield, 1934.

1

Surveyor, Cook And Raw Boundary Rider
The Breaking-in Begins

Australia was not extraordinarily blessed when late in 1911 a young man landed in Adelaide, his mind filled with illusions of a beautiful farm and a rose-clad cottage easily created from land even more easily obtained from a Government which, figuratively, had gone on its knees to implore him to migrate. However, that migration was dictated less by propaganda than by a doctor's views on the probable state of my health if I remained in England a further three years - as well as by two considerations of almost equal importance.

To use a war-time expression, I was a dud. During the three years I attended my last school I was kept in the same class. In history and geography I headed it both in term work and in examination, in all other subjects I was not even an "also ran." I never ran at all.

Not a rich man, my father, nevertheless, paid 100 guineas to article me for three years to an estate agent and surveyor. When serving the articleship I was supposed to pass three examinations which would make me a Fellow of the Auctioneers' Institute, London. But, bless you! despite the expenditure of more money on coaching fees, I wrote a 150,000 word novel on the Yellow Peril, and wrote political letters to the editor of the local paper as from two heated gentlemen, which he published. The doctor was wise in his generation. He pointed a way out. Only fools wrote novels. Only youthful idiots wasted time courting a girl. Send this particular idiot to Australia. Australia will either make or break him.

Followed then a short but intensive study of official immigration literature, elaborate and beautiful, further money spent on a passage, and loh the fool arrived one spring morning in Adelaide.

City of Farmers

During a short stay in the City of Churches I met several young men who had left my home town a year or so before I did, to become Australian farmers. One was a tram conductor; another was a delivery van driver; and a third was preparing for the Methodist ministry. From them I received most peculiar views about farming in Australia; peculiar because diametrically opposed to all those facts and figures and pictures which I had assimilated from Australian literature. My inexperience prompted me to reject such opinions as having been given by men whom this country had proved to be without back-bone.

Those were the years when Australia really and truly was a workingman's Paradise; when there were about two jobs vacant for every man offering. At every station to Pinnaroo. farmers waited on the off chance of persuading a new chum to leave the train to work for him, instead of going on to his assigned destination. It was all comparatively new land, when wheat was selling at 4/2 a bushel, and when machinery, horses and labor were cheap. Another thing which was plentiful was loan money!

My employer was a German, farming five miles out of Pinnaroo, and while we drove to the farm in a springless buckboard, I failed to see any lush pastures, any fat and glossy cows, and not one sweet little rose-clad cottage such as my girl and I had dreamed of in England! The German's house amazed me. It was built of hessian stretched on a bush frame, which supported a corrugated iron roof - all delightfully cool for that time of the year.

Even more amazed did I become at my own quarters - an old 2000 gallons rain-tank turned upside down, and having an opening cut for a door. Within was a roughly made bush bunk.

"It's pretty hot in here just now," remarked my employer. "But you won't notice it because we don't live indoors much."

Fourth Cook

He was right. We did not live indoors much! I was aroused at three o'clock every morning. By the first glimmer of daylight the horses had been fed and harnessed, our own breakfast eaten. We carted hay until eight o'clock, and at nine o'clock, or when it was hot enough to strip, took out a second team to strip till noon. It was eight o'clock in the evening before I had washed up the eating utensils, and nine before I crept to bed.

Alas, like my friends, I had no back-bone. I determined to be a tram conductor, or a delivery van driver, or a minister. And one of the hardest letters ever I wrote was that bitter disillusioned outpouring to the girl in England. All the way out into and back from the Pinnaroo country I saw not one farm which came anywhere near the ideal painted on my brain by that migration literature.

I secured a job in one of Adelaide's largest hotels as "fourth cook."

What a job that was! If only I had stuck to it! The chef was drawing £20 a week. He liked me and offered to teach me all he knew⊠ which would not be in five minutes. We worked from seven to one and from four to seven o'clock. We ate just what we liked, and in less than a fortnight the best was not good enough.

"There will be overtime for all hands tonight," was one day announced. "A Colonel is giving a special dinner to commemorate some battle or other."

"Do you know how to make iced coffee royal?" I was asked by the chef, who had called me into his office. "No? Well, I'll show you. Go down to the bar and get this order. Bring it here."

On the order was rum and vermouth and brandy and twelve bottles of beer. It occurred to me that, vermouth might possibly go into coffee royal, but I was sure that bottled beer did not.

"The beer? That's all right! Put all the order in my office. The beer, you idiot, is for the staff."

Eight tall Cleopatra needles of iced coffee royal went into the private dining room, and about six came out. Beside we cooks, the waiters had a share in the beer, but they had no share in the iced coffee royal. That night the chef slept on the first back landing to his room, the second cook chose the ice chamber for his resting place, while I found the bread table good enough.

Youthful Dreams

Yes, I was mentally deficient to leave that job, but, you see, I was young; I still retained some illusions. I knew that beyond the horizon was adventure and romance. Wheat! Pouf! Gold - opals - cattle - sheep - riding horses - camp fires, and the long, long track a-winding.

The door to this alluring world was shown me by an advertisement which read:

Boundary Riders Wanted for Northern Stations.

Apply Younger, Jones and Co.

"How long have you been in the country?" asked the poker-faced secretary to a pastoral company.

"Two months, sir."

"Oh! Can you ride?"

"Yes. I was in the Hampshire Yeomanry."

"Can you kill a sheep?"

"I think I can manage that all right - even if I have to take an axe."

"Oh! I don't think you have enough experience yet to go north as a boundary rider."

"You give me a chance and see," I pleaded.

"Nothing doing. Good day."

At the same time the next day I again applied.

"I told you yesterday that there's nothing doing."

The next day I applied at the same time - with the same result. The following day I was snarled at and ordered to keep out. At the sixth successive application I won.

"Confound you! I'll send you to get rid of you," the poker-faced man actually howled.

Open Spaces

Among pastoral companies there then was a system in vogue of sending young men to cattle and sheep stations, paying their fares, which was deducted from their wages and repaid if they remained 12 months. As a man who had been legally bound to an employer for three years, I discovered in Australia the admirable custom of being sacked or leaving a job at a moment's notice. Here was democracy! Here was freedom!

The hotel manager smiled and gave me advice with the pay envelope. The French-Australian chef swore, then wept at losing a pupil and sent out a coffee royal order which did not contain vermouth and rum - only beer. He gave me a hamper, which must have cost the hotel a fiver, and, standing beside the poker-faced secretary, watched me slide out of Adelaide as though I were Sydney Carton riding away to the guillotine.

The jumbled hills of the Barrier Range were my first glimpse of the Australia which was to become the passion of my life. Broken Hill was then in its heyday, but I saw little of it. for I arrived at eight o'clock and left for Wilcannia on the Darling at ten o'clock on the box of a Cobb and Co.'s coach.

The driver knew and recited every poem written by the immortal Lawson. His father drove coaches stuck up by the Kelly heroes. The coach, the vast, flat saltbush plain, beyond the horizon of which, as the day wore on, the hills sank like blue-black rocks, the immensity of this world of space, all spelt romance. The grooms at the horse-changes set 20 miles apart were the real thing in Texas gunmen, although their clothes recalled bargees. The Topar Hotel situated at the edge of the mulga lands, at which we arrived at dusk, was the original saloon at Dead Man's Gulch.

All that night and until 2 o'clock the next afternoon I rode the box of a jolting coach. No sleep on the train, no sleep on the coach - the people of Wilcannia witnessed the arrival of a stunned youth. Not then did I know that in the Queen City of the West there were nearly 20 hotels, a very fine gaol, and a brewery, and that on Saturday nights one had to elbow one's way along the sidewalks.

Lashed to the seat of a buckboard, I left with the Wanaaring mail at 4 o'clock. Every time the horses stopped I slept; every time they started an iron-hard elbow was dug into my ribs to awaken me. At midnight I was told that here "I got off." Together with the Tearle Station mail and my suitcase I fell off. The buckboard vanished in the blackness of a calm, hot night. The grounds beneath my feet were yet warm, soft, sandy. No feathered bed ever was so welcomed.

And then a voice, drawling and compassionate, said:

"Better get up and have some breakfast. If you stops there the sun'll burn the whiskers off you."

I had arrived at the land of my dreams. The man who had spoken was to be my breaker and my maker. I would like you to meet him in my next article.

ONE QUALITY ONLY—THE BEST

MRS. S. J. BLOMBERY
Proprietress

Late Kadina, Port Broughton and North Adelaide

Arthur Upfield, feeding a tiny kangaroo.

2

On the Track with One-Spur Dick

To One-Spur Dick I owe a debt never to be repaid. Here on Tearle Station, Western New South Wales, set down in the middle of the night by a mail driver blurred into obscurity by lack of sleep, it has been One-Spur Dick's drawling injunction to "Get up before the sun burns the whiskers off you," which woke me to this new world. Fully dressed, I arose from the soft sand beside the track where I had collapsed into unconsciousness on alighting from the buckboard, to observe four men regarding me with amused eyes, "Another parcel post bloke." one observed, as though I were a beetle.

"Yaas. English or Orstralion?"

"What are you, young feller?" inquired a one-eyed, thick-set, whiskery, sun-blackened man, dressed in blue shirt and moleskin pants, and wearing but one draggled spur.

"English," was my reply, as I gazed around me at the stone-built bungalow house and the skirting corrugated-iron buildings. I slept part of the time while I ate breakfast, and retained a dim memory of being escorted by the whiskery man to the men's hut in which I slept that day and night. The following morning, with the others, I presented myself to the manager for orders, and was told to assist the tinsmith. He was making two 4000-gallon iron water tanks, and my work was to hold a hammer-head against which he riveted the curved iron sheets. It was mid-February and the sun was trying. For two weeks I lived in close contact with Blue Evans, a 14-stone Welshman; Mick Conolly, a tall, flashily dressed stockman; Sam, a full-blood aboriginal; Sam No. 2, a half-caste who shot galahs on the wing with a 22 bore rifle; the Wandering Burglar, wife of one Charlie Monger, and the mother of eight children, only two of whom were not half-castes; and One-Spur Dick then the bullock driver.

New Race of Men

Never before had I met such people; never have I met their like away from the Interior. Their language was terrific, saved from crudeness by its artistry.

Their leg-pulling was severe; tempers quick, and fists hard. Their hearts were big; their humor dry, and the standard of general knowledge surprisingly high. The tanks having been made, I was sent as offsider to One-Spur Dick to fetch in the winter wood supply, with fourteen bullocks drawing an ordinary waggon; and during the morning of the first day. when we then were among dense mulga, it occurred to me - how would I get back to the homestead were my companion to drop dead?

The one-eyed driver - he had lost an eye in a fight at Mount Brown - sternly repressed a leering grin and commanded me to use my brain. For half-an-hour I endeavored to do this, my cursed imagination producing vivid pictures of a lost man dying of thirst. Eventually admitting failure to use my brain, Dick said, with grave deliberateness:

"I like a bloke who arsts questions. I got no time for a bloke, be he new chum English or new chum Australian, wot thinks he knows everything and arsts no questions to hide his ignorance. Now you see them wheel tracks? You go and stand in one of 'em with your back towards the waggon." When I had done as he ordered, he said: "Now shut your eyes. Got 'em shut?" Receiving my affirmative answer, he said: "Now you keep your eyes shut and walk in that track for twenty minutes, and you'll knock out your mosquito brain against the store wall."

Here is an illustration typifying the character of this great man. When assured that in me he had a willing pupil nothing was too much trouble to explain; and nothing was ever explained unless accompanied by a lesson which could not be forgotten! He taught me how to bake a damper, how to kill and dress a sheep, how to make horse hobbles, how to ride in the Australian fashion and how to use my fists. He demonstrated that neither bullocks nor mules nor horses understood pure English or pure Chinese, but would pull like the devil when addressed with a proper mixture of all the oaths of both nations, topped up, as it were, by the worst oaths favored by the Afghans.

Talking To Mules

"Here, have a go at 'em," he urged on our first 120-miles trip to Broken Hill with wool.

He stopped the team. I took the eight-foot whip. He climbed up to the top of the mountain of wool and pretended to go to sleep.

I called to the team of sixteen mules. The leaders looked round with bored curiosity. Twice I almost managed to choke myself to death with the whip. When I managed to lash the shafters, they pulled the waggon forward, but the front port of the team, one and all, yawned. Three times I fell flat, tripped by the whip. I played on a simple variation of two bad words, but they were seasoned, hackneyed British oaths, and of no earthly use.

The team was enjoying a quiet siesta while I became very hot.

And then, over them, rushing outward through the quiet bush, roared a flood of language of such artistry as to be unequalled in any other part of the world. The effect was electrical. Sixteen animals, a huge table top waggon and ten tons of wool abruptly sped towards Broken Hill. As the waggon passed, I managed to grab an eye-bolt at its rear, and despite entanglements with the whip, kept with it.

Without using the single near-side rein - Dick scorned such aid, excepting when negotiating the steep hills of the Barrier Range - my chief pulled up the astounded mules as easily as he had started them - with his voice.

Eventually having learned the language, I got on much better.

My memories of Dick are still vivid. I see him trudging beside the team, an old felt hat set back on his head, the one clanking spur, the long-handled whip over his shoulder with the thong trailing along the ground making a snake track. The whip he seldom used; it was seldom necessary. Swags unrolled on the ground, my head towards the fire, which he carefully fed to keep a good light, I read aloud for hours Sexton Blake, and the work of Stanley Weyman and Charles Darwin. Unable to read, his memory was prodigious, his appetite for any quality of food contained between covers insatiable, equalled only by that for beer - when that kind of food was available.

A Lone Job

Three trips we made to Broken Hill that winter, going south with a mountain of wool, returning north with a mountain of cased rations and fencing wire. The two leaders and the two shafters were allegedly broken in. The twelve body mules we broke in on the track. Twice I saw a pair of hoofs presented one foot beyond my face; once the sleeve of my dungaree jacket was torn away.

Towards the end of the trip the team was settling down, but the end of the third trip dictated a change of employment. It so happened that camping at night on the Wilcannia Common we failed, when coming back, to find two of the mules the next morning, and were compelled to go on without them.

I was sent to the Common Ranger to report the matter, and, having done this, I found the team drawn up outside the Globe Hotel, and poor Dick very drunk within.

"Best thing to do is for us to plant him on top of the load, and for you to drive out to town and camp," said the publican. "You can't pull the team out ere."

I thought that the best thing he could have done was not to permit Dick to become drunk. I was no mule driver. I was a new chum. There were four mules which, even then, required our united efforts to unharness and harness. So they shifted the load a little and made a hole in the top of the mountain into which Dick was dumped, and picking up the whip I whistled to the team, uttered some of the Esperanto of the bush, and away we went.

Now we were bound for the Tearle out-station, to reach which it was necessary to cross the dry Parroo River, a few miles out of town. There were two ways of crossing it: over the bridge, or by taking the track twisting down one bank and up the other. Twice before we had come this way, and because Dick feared that the team would be frightened by the bridge rumble, he had chosen the twisting river-bed track.

"Mug's Luck"

Discovering that I was getting along famously, and knowing that this part of the common was as bare of feed as a city street, I determined to push on until Dick regained consciousness. And now there was the white-painted long bridge making me debate which crossing I would take, and before I had made any decision the leaders reached the bridge.

Now they were on it, their hoofs sounding hollowly on the loose flooring. One of the body mules snorted. Now the shafters. now the waggon itself was on the bridge. I clung to the brake handle praying that if they bolted they would draw the waggon over the bridge on my side. And then, when half-way across, Dick roared, and the team instantly stopped.

I looked up. I saw his face peering over the edge of the mountain. His frozen eyes were gazing down, down beyond me, down to the river bed 50 feet below the bridge. The team was halted. Several of the mules were snorting like donkeys. The leaders looked likely enough to turn and rush back. Dick's voice was a faint whisper.

"Go on! gat 'em off the bridge," he implored, incapable of any other thought, and mentally and physically frozen with horror - in a place where angels would fear to tread. Six feet on either side of the waggon was a 50-foot drop!

We would have been across the bridge ere then had he not come to. I was now as windy as poor Dick, who was enduring a nightmare. But with unmeasured luck, although three of the team began to plunge, the leaders pulled straight, as did the shafters.

Once we were clear of the bridge, Dick stopped the team and

very nearly fell down off the load. In Chinese, he described my ancestors back for five hundred years, danced with rage, and rushed away to return to the hotel.

Thereabouts was no place to camp even if I did successfully manage to unharness the team; and, even had I done this, it would have been impossible to harness them in the morning, new chum as I was. There was nothing else for it but to accept the gamble and push on to the out-station single-handed, despite two bads creeks to cross.

Yet babies, drunken men, and new chums seldom come to harm. Taking that team on to the out-station, though was something heroic. But the fellows could not see it. All they could visualise was Dick looking over the edge of the mountain down to the dry bed of the river.

But to One-Spur Dick I owed a thorough breaking-in, the acquisition of a new and up-to-date foreign language, and the opal gouging fever. I came to sit on 370 pounds of opal - but that is another article!

3

Opal Gouging with Big Jack and his Cat

THE six months which I spent under the tutorship of One-Spur Dick did more for me then remove the rawness of a new chum. Those six months did more than physically harden me by dictating rising at dawn, living day and night in the open air, accepting hardship as normal life. The constant travelling over those 120 miles between Tearle Station and Broken Hill banished for ever any longing for city life, and delayed for twenty years the final and compulsory settling down.

After the one terrible period of nostalgia, hastened by the letter from a woman in England in reply to mine describing the illusions of the immigration literature which we had studied together - a letter asking to be released from her vows of fidelity - I found a mental peace never to be described with mere words. In me was born a passionate love for the Australian bush, which will burn until the end; a love stronger than love of family, so strong that even now it threatens to claim me, and to pluck me out of a city.

In this respect I am not singular by a long shot. Cities bore me. Farming country leaves me cold. Neither cities nor the farming country is Australia, the real Australia adequately described only by Lawson. It has been written by literary folk that the great Australian novel will come out of the cities of Australia. Impossible! There are a dozen Melbournes in the world, a dozen Sydneys. There is only one Australia; a virgin, a living Australia, unspoiled by brick and cement, by axe and plough; the Australia which can reveal a thousand facets of beauty.

Lucky the man to be broken in by One-Spur Dick who, when lounging beside the camp fire amid the mulga or on the horizon-wide saltbush plains around Broken Hill, would recite Lawson's poems, name the glittering store which belonged to us, teach a simple philosophy born of soft, warm earth and soft, bright sky.

Jack Musgrove

And lucky, too, the man to live and to labor with Jack Musgrove from Tasmania, who drank hard, laughed hard, fought hard, and worked hard; lucky⊠ when one is feeling the old accustomed world of dependence and bodily comforts and habit slipping away far beyond the skyline of a new world of independence, self-reliance, astounding interest, tolerance and content.

"Let's go opal-gouging for a spell," urged Jack Musgrove, six feet three inches in his socks -   when he wore them, which was seldom - three feet wide, a face like Atlas, and a fist like a ham.

Go? It was impossible to do anything else. We demanded our cheques at five o'clock one afternoon, and could not wait until the morning to start away. Twenty-one miles we tramped that night with our heavy swags, water-bags and billies, and Marie Lloyd clinging to Jack's neck.

The real Marie Lloyd would have loved Jack Musgrove as much as did that black and white cat who rode him like Sinbad's Old Man of the Sea. Jack's love affairs provided a mine of doubtful anecdotes which he would relate with winks and nods and thumb-jerks, after the great Marie's inimitable fashion.

And wherever Jack went, the cat was sure to go.

At this time White Cliffs had passed its high watermark of production. Like Mount Brown and Tibooburra, the gold-fields not far distant from it. It was a poor man's show, never being taken over by powerful companies.

In the nineties men went to White Cliffs, dug out pockets of opals, sold their stuff to German buyers, rushed to Sydney, Melbourne or Adelaide; for a space lived at the millionaire rate, and then went back to dig up a second pocket; to repeat the process and find a third, and even a fourth, pocket.

Mug's Luck

Naturally, that was before my time. It would be! Twenty-six pounds an ounce was paid for some of it, and when Queen Victoria declined to wear opals and British fashion slavishly followed suit the harems of India provided a fresh market.

Save for investment, I see no beauty in diamonds, and but little in rubies and sapphires in comparison with the flickering green and blue and yellow and red fires in the heart of an opal. Neither did Jack Musgrove. He had opals in a shammy hung from his neck, which he loved almost as much as he loved Marie Lloyd; stones with which he would not part when years later he tramped for work, the soles of his boots gone, his gunny sack empty, and with not one flake of tobacco to press into a cold and empty pipe.

Opal lights are sunsets; diamonds ice.

At White Cliffs, it was as easy to start opal gouging as to pay a Chinaman five pounds for a pack of cards, and to receive from him five shillings for every card "got out" in solitaire. From an urbane celestial we hired picks and shovels and windlass gear.

For a sheer gamble opal gouging stands alone. You may strike a pocket just under the surface, or take over an abandoned shaft and strike a pocket after continuing it downward one foot.

We selected a site not far distant from an old partly wrecked hut which we utilised as a camp windbreak. I used to wonder what kind of a man built it and first lived in it, and at night I used to fancy hearing the heavy tread of men about it.

Swearing Fund

The weather was hot, being the month of March, but what cared we for heat and flies and the duststorms? Had we been expected to work for others like we worked for ourselves, Musgrove, I am sure, would have started a revolution. He sank the shaft. I labored at the windlass. Marie Lloyd lay stretched in a little stone-made sun-shelter erected specially for her, from which at times she would saunter to the shaft edge and look down to be assured that Jack was not asleep or gone on a journey.

Down went the shaft, foot by foot. Father Ryan came one morning to ask how we fared. He knew more of geology than all the geologists in Australia. Round-faced, thick-set, bespectacled, he lived among his flock which included every living soul, whether he was Christian or heathen, or had no religion at all.

"Don't be swearin' so down there," he commanded Jack, then in the bowels of the earth. "Don't be sayin' who the, what the! Just say, Who to that? Brevity be the soul of wit, me bhoy. I always fine a man a penny for every swear word I hear him say."

"Oh! is that you, Father Ryan?" Musgrove shouted. "Good day to you, father. Hey! Arthur! Slip across to the hut and dig out a fiver from me swag! Give it' to the reverend gentleman on account of me swearing fines."

"After, afterwards, me son," Father Ryan requested me. To Jack: "An' hows things down there? Any luck, yet? Come on up, and let me have a look-see."

I wound up Jack in the bucket, and Jack lowered Father Ryan, foot by foot, while he examined every square yard of the four walls.

"Ye might be finding a trifle by going deeper. But it's not impressed that I am," he said, when finally he reappeared. "Well, what the ⊠ ẗemarked Jack conversationally. To which Father Ryan chuckled and said:

"I think I'll be after reminding you of that fiver, me son. It won't be long before you will owe me another, I much fear.

A Lucky Charm

So we labored, sinking a new shaft; and when we had sunk it about ten feet there arrived at our camp two new chums. They were dressed in ready-made suits, starched collars, and cloth caps. They had left their suit cases at one of the hotels, hired a pick and a shovel, wanted to dig somewhere, and would bring out a windlass the next day. Where could they dig?

We were eating morning lunch in the shade of the old hut. They accepted a pannikin of tea, and yet were anxious to get to work. Musgrove suggested the hardest piece of ground within fifty miles; a place but a few feet beyond the hut doorway, beaten and tramped into almost solid rock by countless boots.

Then went to it.

 "Bet you a quid the bloke takes off his collar within two minutes." said my companion, referring to the one who began to use the pick.

 It was quickly evident that those two were miners. That they hailed from Yorkshire was evident, too. That they had arrived at Adelaide on the *Orsova* they told us.

I won the bet, for the pick man did not take off his collar before the expiration of the time limit. He Ioosened a square of earth and his mate shovelled it away. Still wearing his collar he began on the second layer of rock-hard earth.

Then his pick crashed through what sounded like a bottle. A roar from Musgrove stopped the pick descending again into the ""bottle. As though we were financially interested, we showed them how to lift a pocket of wonderful opal, for which a German buyer paid £377!

So, stunned by their fortune, they left White Cliffs without even thanking us. But they recovered a little in Adelaide, from which city they sent both of us ten pounds; said they were leaving by the *Genova* on her return trip, and wished us luck.

"Blast opal gouging!" Musgrove shouted when he was sure that Father Ryan was not within hearing. "Let's get back to the station."

"Do me," I agreed. "I'm wanting a holiday badly."

Arthur Upfield with his two camels.

4

Dire Tale of Goanna and Two Camels

On Mr "If"

HAVE you ever noticed that the sum total of a man's life may be expressed by one short and simple word? Take the failure - Mr If. If he had not done this or that, he would have been such and such. Then there is the man, stolid and solid both physically and financially. Mr Yes is unable to bow, he is so solid and stolid. He is the antithesis of Mr No. poor and starving, weak-chinned and watery-eyed. The difference between these two is that Mr Yes never accepted the negative answer, and Mr No could never do ought else but accept it.

Success in life depends wholly upon the ability to accept the little word "no," or the ability not to accept it. Were I a normally intelligent person, I would have grasped this profound truth when, as described in another article, I got my first bush job, because I would not take "no" for an answer.

After a further exhibition of this gift of stubbornness which, of course, was rewarded with success, I deserve flogging every Monday morning for not making the refusal to accept "no" an unbreakable habit.

When Strike-a-Light George told me there was a vacancy on the vermin fence surrounding a pastoral company's holdings of about one and a half million acres, I said that that job was mine. And because I said it, it was so.

The manager was short and plump and fiery, but, kindly enough, he pointed out that my bush experience was far short of that necessary for the work for which I asked.

The next day when I applied, he said: "I told you yesterday why I won't give you the job."

The third day, he said: "It is no use bothering me."

The seventh day he yelled: "Oh, curse and doubly curse the fools who permit new chums to enter the I country! You'll go and get bushed or the camels will roll on you, and I'll have to send out search parties, and waste my time and write reports! Get out! Get out I tell you! Go to the job and be damned. If ever I see you alive again I'll sack you."

Solitude

"Strike-a-Light!" was the only strong expression ever used by the tall, gaunt man who showed me the 78-mile section of rabbit fence I was to "ride." His section of about 80 miles was further on, and, each fully equipped with a riding and a pack camel for transport, it was not with regret that we parted.

Strike-a-Light was born tired, and he will never die because he will be too tired to do so. He was so tired that he loathed cooking, abhorred washing and reading. In one respect only was he energetic. He never grew tired of grousing. He groused at the most beautifully browned and cooked damper ever I made. When I asked him what was wrong with it he said:

"I always like my damper perfectly round."

Having parted from Strike-a-Light, I faced the bush alone, thrown entirely on my initiative, beyond policemen and ambulances, sign posts and water taps.

After but a slight apprenticeship to the Australian bush. I was about to be tried before Judge Solitude and a jury of two camels, prosecuted by Mr I-told-you-so, and defended by Mr Pride. The trial occupied, to my credit I still think, fifteen months.

Day after day - and never a human voice but my own! Night after night lying on a stretcher beneath a mulga tree, watching the stars and the moon and the clouds, if any; imagination stirring waving nitwits in a dingo park, nerves shocked by the terrible scream of a curlew. Fighting a way along the fence in a dust storm, listening for camel bells to ascertain which direction they took when freed, fearful always of possible accident which, in those conditions, would have but one result. Little matters, one and all, to be laughed at today!

Waiting Bush

I came to regard the Bush as do the blacks. To me it was, and still is, a watching spirit waiting;   waiting for a lonely man to make one slip to claim him for its own. Then I regarded the Bush as a dreadfully malignant spirit; but, with the passage of the years, it gradually changed to one of placid maternity, calmly waiting to take me back, whispering in the trees, singing in the sand.

"Dust thou wast, and dust thou shall become."

The loneliness was less felt when I began again to practice novel writing, and still less when I bought for ten shillings a wall-eyed cattle dog, called Hool-em-up. He had formerly belonged to a man who had a passion for dog fights, and at every opportunity urged this beast to violence. One day, however, the owner of a kelpie sheep dog overheard the cattle dog's owner sooling him to fight, resulting in the dog owners themselves fighting, with ill results to the "sool-em-on-er."

To obviate further unpleasantness, the "sool-em-on-er" re-christened the cattle dog Hool-em-up, and, consequently, it was only necessary for him to shout: "Come here," and yell; "Hool-em-up" to precipitate a dog fight.

That dog might have been good at heeling cattle, but he was no good at catching rabbits or kangaroos. Yet what he lost in "toe" he made up in determination. Once started he went on until the rabbit reached a burrow or a hollow log, or the kangaroo reached Queensland or South Australia!

Always did he scout ahead, unless chasing something, which was about twenty times in the hour. He would suddenly stop to glare at something with his one eye, his one ear pricked - the other, the owner of a licked dog had shot off,   his tail stiff and his hackles raised. Then off he would go with murder in the timbre of his yelps and quite unconcerned by the three-cornered jacks in his feet. But never did he bring anything back from the chase.

Where the fence crossed the dry Parroo, that alleged river was two miles wide. Nothing, of course, grew on it other than spindly, spiny rubbish. The ground was cracked like mosaic work-cracks many feet in depth and sometimes six inches in width. Heaven help the man caught there when the flood waters, instead of rolling along, rise up from the bowels of the earth.

Goanna Chase

And on this country, Hool-em-up must needs chase a goanna which, to this day, I swear was yards in length. When the dog first sighted the land alligator, he was ahead. With interest, two animals and a man watched the race, an interest which increased when the goanna, instead of climbing a fence post, or ducking down one of the cracks, left the fence and circled back, passing us about one hundred yards distant.

The camels stopped, and I waved my hat and cheered. Hool-em-up ran well, but the goanna took matters calmly; until it hit the fence, from which it rebounded with astonishing velocity.

No longer calm, with Hool-em-up in sight of his only victory, the goanna ran along the fence toward us. At their approach the camels became frightened. The pack camel charged between the riding camel and the fence, thus leaving her mate to meet the charge.

Like a ray of dark green light, the goanna thought only of escape from the slavering jaws but two feet astern. It appeared as though; when yet several feet away, the reptile sprang off the ground to reach the riding camel's near shoulder! There was no passage of time between then and when it was clawing its way up me to reach the top of my head.

Followed an earthquake! It seemed like coming down from a balloon and seeing the four legs of each camel spread outward as though they were dun-colored beetles. On awakening I found myself on the wrong side of the fence; and, enclosed in a circumference of one hundred feet, was scattered everything which those two camels habitually carried. They were not in sight, but Hool-em-up was there; peacefully sleeping in the shade cast by a fence post.

What a mess! Here in a ten-by-ten mile paddock in February! Fortunately, I knew that the vermin fence made the southern boundary of the paddock and that in the south-east corner was a dam and two stockmen in their hut.

It was then that Counsel at my trial began argument. Mr I-told-you-so rose to say that I was an absolute failure. Then Mr Pride arose to say that failure was not yet proved. Judge Solitude, like Brer Rabbit, said nothing.

Tracking

So, most rashly, with the undamaged water-bag filled from one of the water drums, I began to track those camels. By dusk I had followed them barely six miles, and would not have reached that far had not the country bordering the Paroo been soft and sandy.

The night was spent on a clay-pan that recalled a doctor's advice to sleep on a billiard table to cure insomnia. The fool! Daylight the next morning found me hungry, but fed with hope of catching up to the camels beyond the next of the eternal sand ridges. On I went, noting how Hool-em-up appeared to be running faster this day, yet never losing sight of the tracks.

About, two o'clock, when I was at fault in hard mulga country, the manager drove up in his buckboard, accompanied by a black boy driving two extra horses. Looking at me, as a doctor might look at a dying victim, he said: "Better get up."

Relating what had happened, I pointed out where last I had seen the camels' tracks. "Oh! You followed them to there," he said, wonderingly. "I thought you were just walking about admiring the scenery!"

He ordered the black boy to hobble the spare horses and then ride to a clump of cabbage trees I had pointed out, from which he was to track and bring back the camels. No longer angry, the manager assisted in making a fire on which the billy was boiled. The black boy presently returned with the camels, and we all went back to the scene of the disaster, where, after a little while, everything again became orderly. When he was about to drive off, I said to the manager:

"I suppose this means the sack?"

"I have never sacked a man in my life," was his reply. "When I want to get rid of a useless man I set him to work scrubbing floors. Just now the floors at the homestead don't need scrubbing."

With a twinkle in his eyes he drove away.

And Judge Solitude smiled at the prisoner.

Arthur Upfield with his camels, about 1926.

5

Tramping by the Darling

INTO my young blood insidiously was creeping the wanderlust. After all the money spent on me, money wasted, deliberately I turned my back on my profession, flung away the opportunities of youth, became only too anxious to hear ever more loudly and to see ever more clearly the spirit of Australia and its many alluring voices.

To observe a ridge of sandhills was to wonder what lay beyond them. To watch the shimmering mirage transforming a gibber plain into a dream of fairy islands and spires and minarets floating on a palm-fringed lake was to inflame my imagination to the point of ecstasy. Perhaps it was the sense of freedom, both physically and spiritually, the knowledge that, should I want to look beyond the sandhills and peer beyond the mirage, there was nothing but my two legs and a water bag to prevent me.

Unlike a child bored with too many toys, unlike a man satiated with lore, unlike a man lost because he has no more worlds to conquer, the man smitten with the wanderlust can never, never grow bored or satiated or lost by too much travel, too much freedom.

The development of the wanderlust in me unfortunately occurred when there did not exist the fear of unemployment. There was always a job on the next station on a farm, and in a city factory, it is unlikely that such conditions ever again will exist; for it was based on a spurious prosperity brought about by almost unlimited cheap money.

Pushing A Bike

As thousands did before us, and as men are still doing in these days of depression, I asked for my cheque instead of orders one bright morning in May, and a week later an eager young man pushed a loaded bicycle out of Wilcannia.

It is surprising how much weight a bicycle will carry. It is surprising how easy it is to push a loaded bicycle. It is even more surprising to feel the joy of travelling beside one of the inland rivers, in May. One's lungs breathe an air that intoxicates: one's eyes are freshened and strengthened by the limitless carpet spread beneath the gums and the box trees, woven by the springing wild carrot, parsnip and buckbush: one's ears are appreciative of the wild's music, fish jumping in the river, the cries of galah and cockatoo and kookaburra, swan and pelican and crane. The crows seem to be less malevolent, the smiling bush welcomes instead of waiting to pounce.

And there is ever a gamble on what the next cook will be like. Will he be generous or mean? For every cook who has turned me away with nothing but a snarl, there have been ten who gave me a "fair issue," and about three who offered me as much as I cared to take.

An outstanding character was Rainbow Harry, so named because of his love of highly coloring his dishes. He was a big man with grey eyes and a full beard as white as the moleskin trousers he wore. At our first meeting he had me at a decided disadvantage. He was standing on a doorstep, and the effect of this enhancement of his height above me will be understood by any salesman. The cook who can look down on the applicant for tucker is placed as the great man who sits at a table set at the farthest end of a huge room.

In The Bag

NOT so foolish as to offer a cook money, I suggested to Rainbow Harry that, perchance, he could give me some flour. The request made him grow one foot taller, made his eyes stand out from his face, and his beard stand out from his chest.

"What? Flour? I can't get enough flour to feed the hands," he shouted, to add with astonishing softness, "Give us your bag."

When he brought me about twenty pounds of flour, I found it easier to suggest that a little tea and sugar would not come amiss.

"Tea? Sugar? Think a station's got nothing else to do but feed tramps?" was the roared question, to be followed by the soft request, "Give us your bags."

Some four pounds of sugar and two pounds of tea duly appeared in my calico ration bags.

I thought of meat, for I was tired of fish.

"Stiffen the crows! D'you think I'm running an abattoirs? Think I can supply every tramp humming on me with meat?" was the shout preceding the whisper. "Give us your, bag."

At least thirty pounds of uncooked mutton was handed out, and with a wink and a grin Rainbow Harry wished me adieu. It appeared that his generosity would have made bankrupt any station had he not been curbed by the manager: and his loud and indignant denials of what tramps thought him to be were obviously intended for the manager's delight.

Fearing for the frame of the bicycle, I yet managed to get the load to the shearing shed one mile up river, where in the shearers' kitchen, I found the usual assortment of men resting from their labors of wandering about. There was Butch, undoubtedly understudied by Wallace Beery. During the two days I camped here he never wore anything other than trousers and singlet. He had never worn boots for years. There was Musical Treloar, who played his violin by the hour - even played it while he tramped. There was the Man from Snowy River, who, in appearance, was a greater villain than Butch: a vast man called Pompey George, and a little, dapper, blue-jowled man named Jake the - , but what the something was I did not know until later. It was not included in the introduction.

His Measure

It was Butch who told me that I need not cook this evening, as dinner was ready. It was the Man from Snowy River who enquired if I was "All right" for tobacco. And it was Jake who stepped to within a few feet of me most offensively to eye me up and down. Took his time, too, like a French peasant contemplating the purchase of a cow.

"How much?" enquired Butch unsmilingly.

Jake circled me, his lips pursed, his eyes screwed into pin points.

"Come on," urged the human gorilla. "How much? A bloke 'ud die of fright waiting fer you to make up yer mind."

"Seven feet two and a half," Jake replied at last, adding decisively, "Yes, must add that half inch."

With that he moved back to the great fire where he had been engaged in grilling a half side of mutton into chops and fillets. Butch, also retiring, I turned to Pompey George, whose measurements were much nearer to Jake's estimate than mine.

"What's he trying to guess? My height?" I demanded irritably.

Pompey George was exceedingly attractive when he grinned. He said, "No. Not your height - your drop." Observing mental sluggishness, he explained: "The little chap is Jake the Hangman. Was hangman once in England. Pulled out when he had to attend to a woman. And he can't break the habit of estimating a man's proper drop."

Here, as elsewhere, when bush tramps foregather, Socialism was practised as it is preached. There was none scheming to make a fortune, or even a comfortable living out of the underdog. Despite outward appearances, these men were carefree and in many respects, admirable. They made me welcome to the cooked food as though it were my right, and provided a menu of grilled mutton and baked cod, feather-weight damper and strong tea.

When packing up preparatory to pulling out, Pompey
George asked if he might accompany us, and, because of his
attractive smile and cleanly habits, I agreed. Despite the frosts he
bathed in the river morning and night. He carried three shirts,
enabling him to put on a clean one every night, I say night
advisedly, because no self-respecting swagman would carry pyjamas.

On The Warpath

Pompey George had one fault, always looking for a fight. Never
did a man so love a fight as did he, and never was a man less
capable of engineering a situation to produce cause for a fight. I
came to see drovers and bullock drivers with ironbark faces and
ironstone fists on their very best behavior in his imposing
presence; for a man whose height is six feet three and whose
width is about a yard surely does possess an imposing presence,
when assisted by yellow hair, violet eyes, and a Rock of
Gibraltar chin.

"If there are any likely looking fellers in this shanty we're
coming to, never you be backward in coming forward," he
said, when we sighted a bush pub between the grey and red
trunks of the giant gums forming a two thousand miles long
avenue which ran by the river.

There were several hard, poker-faced men in the bar, but
nothing happened, and, on our way again, Pompey reproached
me. "You might have started something," he complained. "I
haven't opened my chest for months and months."

Alternately pushing the weighted bicycle, we camped
wherever we pleased; if the weather threatened, in a shearer's
hut, if it were fine and cold, then beside a roaring fire on the
river bank. The fish we caught and grilled on wire netting. The
ducks we bought from ancient fishermen or traded tobacco for
with the blacks. The men we met : how Dickens would have
loved them.

Pompey's Entertainment

We both had plenty of money. We never stayed at a hotel longer than to take two drinks, and, at one hotel, I gave Pompey George his long desired chance. An obnoxious person called me a Pommy, with extras, and although I have played in a soccer team calling themselves with pride "The Pommies," this occasion produced anger.

But before I could get going. I was swept aside by Pompey George, sent flying out through the door. The building proceeded to rock on its foundations, and from doors and windows, and from every crack, poured the yells of men and the dust deposited by countless sandstorms. Men came out of the door one by one as though blown out by an explosion. One issued through a window, bringing the frame with him. Some enjoyed it, others appeared disinterested. Pompey's entertainment cost him three rounds of drinks and two pounds for damages.

For a week he behaved with the irresponsibility of a man in love, and then, as wonderful day succeeded wonderful day, he gradually became his old self - quietly humorous, even tempered, sometimes pensive. For an hour or more he would gaze into the heart of a fire, without speaking one word. Now and then Latin phrases would escape him, and once he discoursed on a cricket match played in the park of an English country mansion which seemed to indicate that he was not one of the gardeners.

There was quite a number of men in the bar of a wayside hotel between Cunnamulla and Wanaaring when we entered it late one afternoon. Outside were two bullock teams and a drover's outfit. We had been there about half an hour when one of the bullock drivers who was the worse for wear deliberately upset my glass.

Here, thought I, was a golden opportunity for Pompey George. I began to discuss the subject of the spilled drink. Began is correct, for I never finished it. An iron-hard fist sent me back against the wall. Oh, Pompey, where art thou? Pompey was outside, and I got the father of a hiding, which was thoroughly deserved.

All the way to Wanaaring, George grumbled and growled because I was fool enough not to have been sure he was present. As though I would have started the play if I had not been sure. When we finally parted, I took a scrub cutting job, and heard no more of him until informed quite recently that he had fallen in Palestine. What a man!

There are worse jobs than cutting scrub - but of that anon.

6

Fighting A Thirst-Mad Mob

JUST fancy going to work by the same train or tram six mornings in every seven, starting work at the screech of a hooter, and working under the watchful eyes of a foreman until the hooter screeches again to knock off! If that has to be done to enjoy the pictures and the beaches and other luxuries, then such joys will never be for me.

In a former article I mentioned appreciatively the Australian custom of being sacked, or leaving a job, at a minutes notice! How irksome it must be for both employer and employee to have to wait even a full day before parting company!

No, no! A hooter would send me mad. So would a foreman. Which is not to say that hooters and foremen are not necessary evils, for without both, many men and women could not work at all. As an Inspector on a Government Fence once said: "Men can be divided into classes: men who can't work unless the boss is looking at them, and men who can't work if the boss is looking at them."

When he said that, I sat down and did nothing until he had cleared off. You see, there are so many kinds of work in the bush at which a man must be trusted to do a fair thing. If he is a born slacker, he will not last long, and will be "Put on tramp" as he should. And here it is that we come to the second Australian custom I hope never to see die out: the mutual spirit of give and take.

I personally do not know the station where the Arbitration Court's ruling regarding hours is strictly adhered to. There never was any necessity to give a ruling laying down the number of hours to be worked in one week. In the first place, no station could be run with men starting and stopping work at fixed hours. In the second place, the old custom of give and take was quite satisfactory both to squatter and man.

It is the rule that men living near the homestead gather outside the office at 7.30 a.m. to receive orders for the day. The work set out seldom cannot be performed later than four o'clock. I have been set work that has been done well and comfortably in two hours; and had "asked for" further orders for that day, if I would have been considered a nuisance. Consequently, no man rightly can feel annoyance if he is asked to do urgent work at seven o'clock in the evening.

Two Wells

There was certainly the practice of give and take at Two Wells, in the south-west corner of Queensland, a place then of magnetic attraction to countless animals and birds. Placed in the middle of an unnatural dust heap having a diameter of half a mile, the two wells were sunk within one hundred yards of each other. In one, the water was as salt as that of the sea; in the other, it was almost fresh.

A windmill raised the fresh water, and a petrol engine pumped up the salt water. Both wells supplied one set of reservoir tallies that fed a line of troughing in each of the converging three paddocks and, because of the number of stock and wild things watering here, both wells were worked hard.

Nearby was a bush shed and a wind-break protecting three tents. A humorous, ancient, wild-eyed and wild-haired Irishman acted as engineer and cook and sheep skinner.

It was the business of two scrub cutters to lay a ribbon of scrub branches across the path of the sheep flocks on their way to and from water; for only at the far ends of the paddocks was there left a little ground feed, the object of this being to prevent drought-weakened animals travelling eight or nine miles to water and eight or nine miles back again the next day to feed. . .

Tune, six o'clock in the evening on a hot, still January day. Temperature well above the century. In the vicinity of the troughs, thousands of strutting galahs and cockatoos; above the troughs a constant whirring of wings and a babel of noise. No emus were present, for they had taken their all at noon. Here and there, in the near distance, solitary kangaroos were sitting up, suspiciously regarding the camp and the troughs at which they must drink or perish.

Further away little spurts of dust rose to hang motionless above the dust heap, flung upwards by bounding fleas which presently resolved into swiftly arriving 'roos. Of rabbits there were none. A heat wave with a shade temperature of 119^0 had killed them all.

"I wish to Gawd it would 'blow," growled Paddy, observing how the kangaroos' dust drifted not at all. "Why they don't put an engine on to that fresh water well beats me. Got to use both wells to maintain a supply, and the mixture about 90 salt and 10 fresh. Them poor critters walkin' miles and miles to get a drink of sea water in this heat! The dam mill hasn't gone all day. I had to shin up the mill and turn the fan wheel to get enough water for us."

Brown Clouds

There was no hint of Ireland in Paddy's voice, but the brogue was strong in Irish Muldoon. In his youth this man of middle height and large girth had studied for the priesthood, and if ever you have been cornered in a bar and compelled to listen for anything up to two hours to light hours and densities, magnitudes, and angles and systems, then you have met Irish Muldoon. He had long forgotten all that, as known by Sir James Jeans!

"Tanks full?" he asked in that soft, pleasant voice of his, nothing being further from his mind than the celestial bodies when he was sober.

"They could be fuller. The mobs are coming in now." From north of west and from due south, steadily rising brown clouds of dust rose into the red-flecked bronze of the sky, each cloud whirled upward by the close-packed lines of travelling sheep. The vast dust columns marched toward us with the steadiness of tramping giants - that to the south mushrooming into a cloud which had the precise aspect of a water cloud, snow white, its western face tipped with plnk by the westering sun.

Now we could see the dull grey lines leaving the scrub at the foot of those gigantic dust columns. The western one blotted out the sun which, striking upon that to the south, painted the column with ever moving splashes of crimson. Louder and louder became the sound of eager "baaings"; faster and faster moved the leaders towards the water which had lured them for so many weary miles. And presently was added the low rumble of thousands of hoofs, churning up the dust that hid the almost countless followers. "I suppose we had better get going?" suggested Irish Muldoon. We set off each to a line of troughing.

Flood of Wool

Now Paddy had slaved all day at tending the engine and the pumps; skinning dead sheep, and cooking for the camp. Save for the midday hours, Irish Muldoon and I had swung an axe against tree branches in the scorching sun. Yet there was no suggestion made that this was as after working hours; that we were not paid for the task ahead of us. For thus was not a matter between the owner of the run, who lived in England, and ourselves. It lay between ourselves and poor, helpless, water-famished animals!

Your bushman may be rough and hard, he may never grease his hair or manicure his nails; he may always spend his cheque in a pub or indulge in every city vice when on holiday, but he is a sentiment. I cuss with animals.

Here at Two Wells, night after night, we each arrived at the water troughs with the sheep. Outward from the troughs spread the flood of wool. More densely rose the now stationary dust columns merged by close proximity into one. Here was a mad, straining, trampling, moaning surge of flesh and bone and wool pressing to get at the water; with here and there mounds of wool heaving above, the general level, each mound marking the place where a sheep had fallen and was being trampled to death.

Dust-choked and heated, we scrambled from mound to mound to rescue the fallen. Then to the troughs to seize a foolish sheep which had been pushed into it, and was blocking the flow of water.

So it went on. The leaders, having distended their bellies with brine, forced their way through the streams of arriving sheep to take position several hundreds of yards distant where they waited stolidly chewing their cud. With the passage of time the weaker sheep arrived - sheep which lurched and staggered, glassy-eyed, gaunt despite their wool, their mouths dry and as hot as fire.

They went down in dozens in the scramble, poor beasts that when lifted moved strengthless legs frantically to get them to the water. And having drunk and drunk they lay down, with bellies distended, close beside the troughs, refusing to get up, or to stand I up when lifted.

Gradually the dust thinned. Behind the halted leaders massed sheep in their hundreds, heavy with water, tired to the point of exhaustion by that long walk. About the troughs the press of sheep ceased to reveal vacant spaces. All about were sheep lying down, muzzles resting on the ground, eyes, closed or almost so. Others lay dead, their last ounce of waning strength used up, expended in effort never to be rewarded.

Spectres

And now through the hanging dust came the spectre of drought. Strange shapes that moved a little forward, fell, moved again, fell and moved onward yet again, tongues lolling from scorched mouths, some with an eye or both eyes plucked out by the crows. A little rest, and then one more effort; another little rest, and one, oh! just one more effort, to drink and drink and drink.

There was Irish Muldoon straddling sheep and walking them to his trough. There was Paddy screaming oaths and curses, and carrying water in a tin to pour down the throats of sheep doomed to death. He said he did it to save as many as possible, to lighten the work of skinning the dead ones the next day. The liar!

Evening after evening the western sky was like the wall of a slaughter house. Day after day showed the fiery heat of the torturing sun. After the sun had set the afterglow red denied this field of horror, the standing water-filled flocks, the individual sheep lying down between them and the troughs, and between the troughs, out along the paths the flocks had taken from the scrub lines.

Far and near, black dots moved sluggishly about dun-coloured mounds - crows feasting on the bodies of animals which had failed to come in. Kangaroos were creeping closer on all fours. Others were hopping short distances. Yet others were sitting up waiting, waiting for men to leave the water, which they must get or perish . . .

Faces red with dust, perspiration glueing our clothes to our bodies, we would finally go back to camp and pour water over each other. The dusk was deepening, and flocks were lying down close-packed for protection against the foxes. From each flock individual sheep left to drink again, and to return slowly.

Over a pannikin of tea Paddy would curse the squatters for breeding sheep to suffer thus, and, in the natural order of things, Irish Muldoon would uphold the squatters. Their voices would rise high in vocal combat.

And finally we went to bunk on stretchers brought out from the tents, lying on them without covering, listening till long after midnight to the ceaseless cries of the wild that came from the water troughs; to the warning thrump-thrump of kangaroo tails, the snarl of a dingo, the spitting "quex-quexing" of quarrelling foxes. The world was hidden at long last by the merciful darkness.

Arthur Upfield with his donkey team in 1928.

7

When Crabby Tom Ran Amok

I found in my outback life that by far the most important person on any station is the cook! He has it in his power to create for others heaven or hell. For the sky will be bright and energy at full strength after a breakfast of well-grilled cutlets and well-made yeast bread; while life will be dull and not worth living if the cutlets have been grilled to cinders and the bread is more fitted to take the place of putty in window panes.

As a class, all cooks are different. Their tempers are uneven, and one never knows the moment when a cook will tear off his apron, dance on it, raise his hands on high, and depart, swearing that never again will he feed such low, grousing, lazy crawlers.

There was Ted Ellis. No man ever lived who knew more sea shanties than he. These he sang the livelong day - until someone came along who offered him a "taste." It was always the taste that did it. Within an hour, Ellis was heading for the nearest pub.

There was Crabby Tom. Invariably, when he arrived to take charge of a kitchen, he was on the verge of delirium tremens. I say "on the verge," because he would be too drunk to enjoy them, and only when sobering-up did he see things which did not exist.

I first met Crabby Tom when he arrived at a place named Wombra Lake, meaning in the local aboriginal dialect, Big Lake. Just where the lake was I never discovered, despite the fact that then I was riding three paddocks totalling in area something like 199 square miles.

Seeing Things

My fellow stockman was away on a trip, and for some time I had had to do my own cooking, when the boss rang to say that he was sending out a cook on the truck the next day. And during the next day I had visions of beautifully cooked meat and freshly baked, feathery yeast bread. It follows that my interest was aroused when, on sighting Wombra Lake after a long day, I observed a man running round and round the two huts.

Having unsaddled and freed the horse, I was able to give further attention to the sprinter. He was about 60 years old, wore nothing but underpants, and showed remarkable stamina. Now and then he would glance over his naked shoulder, utter a loud yell, and speed up. With the regularity of clockwork he would disappear round the corner of one hut and reappear round the corner of the other, quite oblivious of my presence.

It happened that in the scabbard attached to the saddle I was holding was a .32 rifle, and when he again hove in sight, I allowed him to pass me before firing off the gun and pretending to chase an imaginary horror. With that, Crabby Tom pulled up and came about with rasping breath.

"Did you get him?" he wheezed, hair on end, eyes dilated, teeth bared in a terrible grin.

"Wounded him," I admitted sorrowfully. "But he's cleared out. He won't come back any more. Better come in and we'll get some tea."

"Right! But you keep the gun handy, I ain't no shot. I never killed anythink yet," he said earnestly.

"Leave it to me. Did you bring a drink out with you?" I enquired, desiring to know the amount of the stock, if any.

"No. Old Starlight" - meaning the boss -" took a full bottle off me. Blinking shame, and me dyin' for a drink."

The poor wretch sat on a form against the table in the kitchen, while I got the fire going, and, later, unrolled his swag and made up his bunk. I was in two minds about ringing Old Starlight and giving him my views about dumping a madman on me, when Crabby leapt two feet off the ground, vented an ear-piercing shriek, climbed the table, and swung himself up on to one of the roof cross-beams.

"Look out! It's just behind you!" he yelled. "It'll get you! It'll get you!"

Bedlam

Endeavouring to pay him and allay his terrors, I made tea, and, when he refused to eat or drink, ate a hearty meal, believing that a stormy night lay ahead. And a stormy night it was, too. No doctor handy to give him a shot or two of morphia; no policeman in the vicinity to yell for if Crabby Tom got his hands round my throat, thinking he was strangling a green man with blue hair and red eyes! A situation, indeed, to make one exercise what little brain one might have.

"Look out mate! It's behind you again!" Or; "Shut the door! Can't you see its trying to get in?" Or it might be in stuttering wails: "Bug! Bug!" and he would frantically brush things off his person, or from the beam supporting him.

With a man in such a mental state, pleading and argument are useless. The only efficient method of dealing with such a person, should morphia not be available, is to club him into unconsciousness with a mulga root! But to this method is attached some slight risk of being charged with the crime of murder, because the necessary judgment and finesse are qualities rare in the average peaceable man.

About nine o'clock I gave Crabby Tom half a bottle of pain-killer, but to my disgust it had no effect on him. At ten o'clock I was getting "fed up." At eleven, when Crabby was barricading himself into the fowl house, in company with twenty squarking hens. I contemplated rolling a swag and going away into the scrub to sleep. After all, I was not being paid the handsome sum of 30 shillings a week and tucker, to nurse a lunatic.

Bush Doctoring

However, there are occasions when one has to do small odd jobs without hope of gain, and about midnight I determined to experiment on Crabby with chlorodyne. From five to thirty drops was advised for cases of nervous debility and a hundred other complaints.

Now Dogger Smith once told me without batting an eyelid that he had drunk two full bottles when he anticipated an attack of D.T.'s, and allowing a large reduction of 75 per cent to counter exaggeration, I gave Crabby Tom a whale of a dose. In twenty minutes he had regained normality and drank a pannikin of tea, and ten minutes later he was sleeping in his bunk.

Blessed rest! Exhausted, I lay down to sleep, the two scared cats coming to sleep on my feet as always they did. Peace! Wonderful peace at last! The night so quiet! Aye, a little too quiet. I could hear no sound from Crabby Tom, no snore, not even his breathing.

He was lying on his back. His face was dull grey. His lips were purple. His eyes were shut. There was no movement of his powerful chest. I thought of the looking glass to make sure he was dead. For hours I slapped his face and shook him. For hours I walked him round and round the room. It was full daylight when I collapsed - and he was snoring in healthy sleep.

Mushrooms

But he was cured, and the trouble and fright he had given me were worth it all, for he proved to be the finest cook in my experience.

All cooks have bad feet as well as bad tempers, brought about by standing on hard floors in slippers. A cement floor will cripple a man in no time. Yet to offset this drawback, there is always a job waiting for a good cook even in these days of depression. Cooks, who have to labor seven days in the week, are always scarce; a good cook is as rare as water in the Paroo River.

The day must come when a bushman will have to turn cook, and I found that a knowledge of cooking is no weight to carry, and a trade of value when held in reserve.

My first batch of bread was not a success. There must have been something wrong with the yeast, and after forty-eight hours I baked the dough hoping it would rise in the oven.

Yes, it must have been the yeast. When, in disgust, I threw a loaf out of the window, it cracked a hard clay-pan, star fashion. The second batch was a trifle better, although it had not risen a fraction of an inch in sixty-four hours. In the quiet of the night, feeling like a body-snatcher, I buried about thirty pounds of dough in the ash heap.

And when the hands came in to lunch the next day, the blacksmith said with a grin: "Have you seen them mushrooms out by the ash heap?"

It was the mushroom season, and I have a strong passion for mushrooms, but decidedly it was not the season for that buried dough to rise and shame me.

8

Sandstorm Terror in Sturts Country

Should you desire to see flies - you would be an extraordinary person if you did - visit the north-west frontier of New South Wales. If you would experience real dust storms, and would appreciate sunny Australia, by all means take train to Broken Hill, and from there travel some 200 miles by mail car to Yandama or Quinambie Stations, any time during January and February.

Most certainly you will be tormented by the flies, choked by the dust, and dimmed by the heat. You will never recall the name of Sturt, Australia's greatest explorer, without "living" with him and his companions every minute after he left Cawndilla Lake, which is beside the Darling above Menindee, in January, 1845.

Modern "explorers" who rush around in motor-cars and huge trucks make me smile. When they name pot-holes and ant-heaps as lakes and hills - the mud of the former sucked by a lone prospector, and the elevation of the latter used by a stockman to spy out possible feed for his weary cattle before ever the "explorer" was born - I get that tired feeling.

How I would like to have one in my power and say to him: "Here are two camels and equipment and tucker for a month. You can get water at such and such a bore. The water will be a little salt, but that is neither here nor there. Work along this 22-mile section of dog-proof fence, and don't let me see you for a month. It is unlikely you will see anyone, black or white, but that's nothing, as lots of men go two to three months without seeing or speaking with anyone. Now get going, my son, and crack hardy."

One can so easily imagine the chuckles and back-thumpings among the old-timers of "The Corner."

Sandhills

You face north; it does not matter if you face south, but we will say north; and beyond a narrow flat, covered with low bush and widely spaced wind-wracked mulgas, you will see a huge wave of sand; here topped with a curling sand-cap, there gouged by a giant's scoop. No car ever built could surmount it; it is doubtful if an army tank could make headway up those slopes of fine light-red sand.

Beyond it lies another narrow flat, and beyond that another sand wave, and so on, and for miles and miles, six or seven sand waves to be surmounted with every mile travelled northward. Picture a storm-lashed ocean suddenly petrified, each way 50 to 70 feet high. Save for a panting eagle perched on the limb of a dead sandalwood tree, and a wide-beaked crow or two, no bird life.

The South Australian Border Fence is an everlasting switchback, a netted barrier six feet in height, topped by barbed wire, which takes a man's ingenuity to scale and which balks any animal. Running north-south, it is opposed to the full force of the westerly hurricanes of wind and sand.

"You can have no idea of that region," Sturt wrote to MacLeary in 1845, and with MacLeary, I had no idea of it until the Inspector wrote offering me a job riding 22 miles of that fence. Twenty-two miles! Why, I could do that on my head, I thought. I found that the 22-mile sections were exactly 12 miles too long.

My camels were Martin and Emily. Martin was a staid old gentleman who could not go without a sip of water after two days. Just a sip to wet his cud, or determinedly he would hobble off to the nearest bore. Emily was a gay widow or a placid cow, according to the mood of the moment. When it was really hot, when the ground burned the rubbery soles of their feet, they would go on strike by making for the nearest alleged shade and camp. And when I had removed the loads and got a billy going over a fire, they would get up and come to stand over it, their heads steadily thrust into the uprising hot air and smoke in which, in all that land, there were no flies.

Between their heads would be mine, and the slab of salt meat; and the slab of rock-hard damper, too, because when not thus protected, it was impossible to convey food to the mouth without flies adhering to it. No butter, of course, and frying fat kept in corked bottles!

Heart-breaking

The flies had a liking for canvas, and would blacken the tent used to cover the load on Emily, so that it looked like black American cloth. To escape them meant breakfast before dawn and supper after dark. There were evenings when the camels never moved their heads from the hot air of a camp fire or a rubbish fire until darkness vanquished the flies.

I used to smear a mixture of axle grease and kerosene round their poor eyes. About my head I wore a woman's veil, but firing two such veils with cigarette smoking, I gave the flies best and suffered not silently.

The fence job was the most heart-breaking of any I have attempted. Every little bit of obstruction had to be kept clear of the bottom of the fence to allow the drifting sand to trickle through the netting mesh.

Once rubbish was allowed to collect against that barrier, in no time, where there had been a fence, there would be a sandhill over which dogs and foxes and rabbits could enter New South Wales. With a rake I would remove all such rubbish. The next day a wind storm would sweep from the west millions of football-like, brittle buckbushes. The whole surface would appear to move, sliding eastward to be halted against the fence, to pile up against it higher and higher until tons and tons of dead buckbush would steeplechase the fence into New South Wales. Work undone within an hour; work having to be done again and again!

I have found the fence on the summit of a sandhill twenty and thirty feet high instead of the regulation six feet, swaying in the wind; or it might be lying flat; and all day I have labored to remove successive "topping" of posts and netting. A storm had blown away the summit of that hill, and the next one, or the one after, would build it up again, necessitating rebuilding the fence.

And the wonderful water! How the laundry people would have appreciated it! Arrived at a bore head, the steaming hot water ceaselessly pouring from the angled piping, all that was necessary to wash clothes was to hold them on a stick beneath the gush. No rubbing, no soap required. After the fifth wash you could blow holes through a shirt.

Both sides of the bore drain were sudded with soda and alkalines, and to obtain drinkable water one had to go half a mile down the drain. Even at that point the water was too brackish to make tea; but with plenty of sugar it was possible to drink coffee made with it.

Willy-willy

No wonder that Sturt and his heroic band were dismayed by this land of sand and wind eighty-eight years ago. If the sun rose like Alaska gold; much more yellow than the Australian mineral, it prophesied a day of roaring wind and stinging, choking sand, in which nothing could be done save to crouch in the lee of a pack-saddle - to face the storm was to have one's eyes filled with sand; to turn from it was to have one's face a crawling mass of flies sheltering in the windbreak.

The strangest storm ever I experienced swept across this country one afternoon in November. The day was still. Cigarette smoke rose up in a straight spiral. The camels crouched in meagre shade. Every time I moved out of that meagre shade I became dizzy. In the nearest station homestead they said it was 119 in the shade; proper shade, of course.

Above the sand-gashed horizon rose a long, low cloud having a much greater density than the usual sand storm. At a distance it appeared to hover just above the ground, rolling eastward with the irresistible solidity of a sandhill two hundred feet high, stretching from the north to the south. When it drew near at the speed of a trotting horse, its aspect was much like a terrific, Medusa-frozen sandhill come alive.

It frightened me. In it there seemed to be no possible chance for a human being to breathe. There was no time to pack up and ride away before it. From black, it had changed to dark red, terrifying in its relentless approach, sinister in its silent march. I believe that, had there been a rabbit burrow near, I would have thrust my head down one of the holes; and at the last instant, it was the tent fly beneath which I wormed a way for shelter.

With a gentle hiss, it covered me up, blotted out the sun, created a darkness known by the Egyptians and the Israelites. The darkness lasted for about two minutes. Then the light came back and the sun shone again. Still no wind. Every surface presented by tree branch, the camels, equipment, fence posts, even the fence wires, was loaded with sand precisely as such surfaces in a cold country may be so loaded with snow!

Native Craft

It is a land inhabited by the remnants of a tribe of the great warring Dieri nation, which ousted another in the long ago and settled all the way up the Barcoo delta from Lake Frome to Lake Eyre; the latter named after the explorer, the former after a Captain Frome, once Surveyor-General of South Australia.

Opportunity came to visit Lake Frome with a Dieri native and a half-caste. When we wanted water they would uncover several roots of a needlewood tree, break them, and place beneath the breaks any tin receptacle with us. Then they would fire the foliage, and the fire would drive into the tins from half a pint to, in some cases, over a pint of drinkable liquid.

When near Lake Frome we fell in with a party of natives who could not, or would not, speak English, but who, responded to certain Masonic signs. That mystified Sturt, and it mystifies me to this day. The only explanation appears to be that of coincidence; for the origin of Masonry is comparatively recent compared with that of the sign language of the aborigines.

Anyway, it gained us open sesame, gained for us "official" permission to proceed, without which neither the full-blood nor the half-caste would have gone on.

From the summits of the eastern sandhills on a clear day, it is possible to see the tops of the western sandhills across the mud flats which are designated a lake on all maps. In dry weather, wild dogs may cross by rigidly following their own made pads. At all times, those flats are death traps to both cattle and horses. After a heavy rain there may be stretches of water an inch or so in depth, which last a week or two in winter.

If there be such a place on this fair earth of ours favoured by Satan as his backyard, and it is about Lake Frome and the S.A. Border Fence in summer.

Emily -
a lady
of
moods.

9

Mad Fever of the Skin Game

A man on gold never watches the clock. To him Time does not exist; even food is ignored until the body grows weak from lack of it. The energy of his mind is consumed by the magic of golden dreams from which he is recalled only by waning daylight.. Yet there is no excuse for the prospector on gold working over-long hours and starving himself, for the gold, having been hidden in the ground for countless ages, will not run away.

To the fur-getter Time is very real, ever present at his elbow to nudge him on to ceaseless labor. Instead of watching and anxiously waiting for Time to relieve him of labor, he finds Time always at his heels, always trying to catch up to him, in his mind the ever-present dread that a climatic change will occur to stop the flow of the fur that he is turning into gold.

For every rabbit is a grain of gold, every fox ten grains.

Moss Brown's motto was: Make hay while the sun shines; loaf when it rains. He liked taking Government fencing contracts and on such occasions, in his dictionary, there was not to be found the word "stop." He came out from Broken Hill in a Ford car; the first Ford car to reach Broken Hill, eventually to be converted into a truck. It used to go with leaps and bounds, but I would cross Australia on it today, because, despite the leaps and bounds, it always got to one's destination.

Seeing the countless grains of gold, he asked for a partner. I became it. I say "it" advisedly, because for months and months I was an inhuman machine which knew not leisure, and precious little sleep.

The Trap

It was February when we started work on one of the great surface dams east of Victoria Lake, in the Western Division of New South Wales. We netted the dam water and built trap yards one day when even the crows refused to leave the shade, and the evening of that day found us at opposite corners of the dam, each with a shot gun and cartridges with which to keep the kangaroos from breaking the flimsy netting fence and releasing our catch.

The surrounding country was a Sahara, made so by the passage of sheep and countless animals daily converging upon the water. The sheep now had been moved, for there was but a foot of water remaining, and that foot might be sucked up by the sun in any one hour. Dusk was falling when the first rabbit slipped over the dam bank, without pausing, with terrible determination to reach the water. Another appeared, then two, then four, then a continuous procession. We could hear the faint rustling noise of their passage. One I caught easily when it passed me. and it squealed, seemingly less from fright than from anger at being delayed. When released it continued its journey as though oblivious of the fact that a human hand had snatched it up.

The fence round the square sheet of water was erected about one yard from its edge. Twice on each of the four sides, the fence was fashioned into at V, the point of the V six inches from the water, and at the point of the V was a small hole, cut large enough to permit a rabbit to squeeze through. At opposite angles a V in the fence, pointing outward from the water, led into a large, strongly-built netted trap-yard.

Frantically searching for a way through to the water, a rabbit would enter one of the V's, reach its point, poke its head through the hole, when its twitching nose would be within a few inches of the water it must drink. Thirst burning away suspicion, it would edge further through the hole and drink with half its body beyond the hole. Another rabbit coming behind it, hearing it drinking, would nip it on the rump, whereupon the first rabbit would worm the whole of its body through the V and in order not to wet its foot, it would move to one side of the V where it would have room, and then be imprisoned between the water and the fence. From then on rabbits trickled through the V's like golden drops of grain falling through an hour-glass, and their thirst quenched, their bodies distended with water, there was no going back the way they had entered, save through one of the larger holes in a V leading into a trap-yard.

Truce

I know of no greater drama than that which is enacted in the pit of an almost dry dam at the end of a red hot day where thousands of animals - rabbits. foxes, kangaroos and wild dogs - meet and mix without fear of one another, quenching a thirst which has tormented them for hours, while they crouch in the shade cast by the surrounding scrub; waiting, watching the sun which seemingly never, never will set. From our fence, masked by the darkness, there would come to our ears the ceaseless murmur of scurrying rabbits. The light of a hurricane lamp would show them packed in long lines, drinking at the water's edge, blocking the V's in maddened effort to get through, running along the outside of the fence in thousands, close packed already in the trap-yards where, by morning, there would be 1000 in each.

Stationed a little below its summit of the dam bank, in order to obtain a sky line against the stars, we would observe rising above it, strange, monstrous shapes against the dark sky, shapes unimagined, like a cross between a giant spider and a crab. Kangaroos, ungainly, creeping silently toward the water, unlike the rabbits, their suspicion not swamped by thirst, knowing that man was there, fearing those loud reports of guns, warned by sentinel 'roos.

In the dark, unable to see the gun sight, we shot them or frightened them off; fearing to move from our positions to despatch the wounded animals in case the other might mistake one for a 'roo and shoot▨ which has been done more than once!

Foxes and dogs would cross our sky-line too quickly for action. In any case, they were not a menace to the fence, over which they would lightly leap, and flap noisily as though they would never stop. Perhaps on their way out they would fancy a rabbit, when there would come up out of the pit a roar of scampering feet when thousands of rodents would rush to escape.

One night, after Moss Brown had fired from his position at the opposite corner of the dam, he began yelling, which gave me cause to think he had shot himself. When I called out he pantingly replied. "I shot and wounded a 'roo on the top of the bank, and he rolled down to me, and now he's trying to get into bed with me. He's all hind feet and front claws and teeth."

Slaughter

At that time rabbit skins fetched £2 a 100 in the Sydney auction sales. The Americans and the Belgians were keen buyers, and rabbit skins and carcases were fifth on Australia's export list. In the old countries, the skins were made into beautiful "Arctic fox" and mink furs and coats, and as such were worn by the ladies of Europe and America, little dreaming that on their backs and round their lovely necks nestled the good old Australian rabbit.

When we moved camp to Victoria Lake, then as dry as a dog's buried bone, there was no necessity to use traps of any description. We used to drive the rabbits into the burrows, select a surface warren on soft ground, and block up all the exits. Every runway would be choked with the rodents, so that at most of the holes would be seen the hind quarters of rabbits unable further to get in.

Starting from one exit I would drag them out and kill them as fast as Moss could skin, with a forearm easily breaking the surface crust. Here and there would be an underground chamber, crammed with rabbits, from which other runways would lend out like the spokes of a cart wheel. In this way we would catch and skin 500 rabbits in a morning.

April came, and with April the autumn rains. The rabbits scattered over the country, cleaned out old warrens, and set to work breeding. Moss found another partner, and I bought a truck and equipment of my own and set to working in trapping early in May; The fur fever burned and burned. Skin prices soared to an average of 80 d. a lb. Eight skins to a pound: averaging 19 d. a skin. That winter, for several pounds of beautiful fawn skins I received 116 d. a lb. Seven went to the pound - averaging $14^{1/2}$ a skin. I thought of selling my stretcher and blankets. What was the use of a bunk anyway?

No Pause

At noon every day I had moved sixty gin-traps to fresh ground and had set them. Then back to camp for a hasty meal, and to stretch the skins obtained the day before. At two o'clock, the first visit to the trap line to take out 30/-. Back to camp to prepare fox baits of fat balls dipped in strychnine crystals. Then to cook food, and if time remained, inspect and plan other trap-lines.

At sundown, a hasty meal. When darkness was falling, dragging a sheep's head over the ground to make an easily followed fox trail, and along that trail at 50 yards intervals, laying two baits - two because a fox would have to swallow one to pick up the second.

Then out again on the trap-line. Walk, walk, walk! I had been walking at top speed all day. Now with a hurricane lamp to take more tenpences out of the traps. Nine o'clock that would be and at ten o'clock, one would be at the far end of the trap-line lounging beside a roaring fire, and walking round it, if sleep threatened to conquer the mind. The trap line again, and back to camp at midnight. Into the blankets for four hours, the alarm clock lashed to one's neck, because if set on a box beside the bed, it would fail to rouse.

Four o'clock in the morning, and bitter cold. A drink of strong coffee laced with brandy, a bite to eat, and a cigarette before the dawn lightened the sky. In the half-light of daybreak, ready at the home end of the fox trail, carrying chaff bags to cover fox carcasses from the crows; there at that hour to stop the crows from finding the baits and causing waste of time looking for foxes supposed to have taken them.

The Haul

Here a splash of brown. Over there another. There must be at least four others. Somewhere they are among the short bushes. Walk, walk, walk, quartering the country to pick up 10/-. Ah! Not so bad. Fox skins to the value of £3. Again on the trap-line, picking up the traps and carrying them In bundles to fresh ground, taking out 71 rabbits in that 24 hours. Say £6. Not so good as the day before, but better than the day before that.

It is noon again and the traps are all set on new ground. Confound the sun! Why cannot it stop still for a little while and give a fellow a chance to get his breath? There are those skins to skin on wire bows and the fox skins to peg out on a clay-pan, fur down. At the end of the first three weeks I was weak enough to lie down on the bed just for five minutes rest - and slept for fifty hours. Henceforth. I rigidly kept the Lords Day, and, as a result, worked faster during the week.

The new grass came up. Countless baby rabbits filled the traps, stopping the flow of gold. At the end of June, the foxes mating season started, when the foxes will not eat meat, no matter how carefully served up to them. The problem arose - what did they eat? Solve that, and it would be possible to gather 10/- notes up to mid-September. I shot a fox and held a post-mortem examination to find that it had lived on scorpions and centipedes, and because I was a dud in catching those hibernating pleasantries, I went back to stock work.

But I watched the rabbits with lustful eyes, and followed the skin market reports as eagerly as a lover reading his love's letters. Drought set in, and at the end of two years the skin game was finished. A man said to me: "Let's go to the West. Over there, if the rabbits fail we can go dry-blowing for gold." That very hour we packed up camp and started off for Perth, a journey of 2500 miles. That decision finally produced the novel, *The Sands of Windee*, the plot of which cost three men their lives, and dragged me into the most amazing murder case in the history of Western Australia.

Arthur Upfield's dray with writing desk at left under the lamp, 1930.

10

'Snowy" Rowles, Gay Daredevil

WHEN I had been six months in Western Australia, I got a job - I like this simple, low-brow word - as a boundary rider on the No. 1 Rabbit Proof Fence, which runs from Starvation Harbor, on the south coast, to Sharks Bay, on the north-west coast, a distance of more than 1300 miles. My section began at the Government Camel Station on the Murchison, running southward for 163 miles to the Perth-Kalgoorlie railway.

Here one drove two camels tandem fashion drawing a heavy two-wheeled hooded cart in which, night after night, I continued my writing. A furious thunderstorm or a plague of moths putting the hurricane lamp out of action might interrupt, but no lesser inconveniences did.

Never have I been able to afford the artistic temperament, and in this cart, parked beside the fence track at the edge of dense desert scrub, I wrote my third novel.

Now when a writing job is finished, I suffer a period of mental depression. Having lived for six months or more with a set of characters, the abrupt parting from them leaves a blank in life which is banished only by the slow creation of another set. Some people, I know, invent a plot to suit a set of evolved characters, some dispense with any plot at all, but I must first have a plot, or a central idea, and as my motto is "Originality or nothing" my mind may be occupied for months in a search for an original plot.

The third novel having been accepted for publication in London - it was a psychological study - I determined to produce a second Napoleon Bonaparte mystery story, in which Bony would be given a case worthy of his quite ordinary intelligence but extraordinary bush lore.

Germ of Idea

You who read this, will agree, I think, that exceptionally few novels are original in plot. Ninety-nine per cent harp on the old themes invented by the ancients - the eternal triangle, sex with or without jam, lunacy and sadism, and then more sex. In comparison murder yarns are clean and healthy.

Wilkie Collins was about the first to lay down certain rules for a detective murder-mystery, and ever since his day, novelists have slavishly followed his rules. In the first chapter, there must be a grisly corpse; in the second, a detective arrives on the scene. In the third, the detective discovers the inevitable clues, which he follows throughout the remainder of the book.

All this amply satisfied our grandfathers, but surely it should not satisfy us! Originality is the breath of life, and I would go down upon my stiffened knees to the man or woman who could invent a new sin.

So it was that I determined to commit a fiction murder to take place long before the story opened. There would no particle of a corpse in existence. And then my detective. Bony, should, from the very Sands of Windee, prove that a man had been killed, how he had been killed, and who killed him. In my now novel there should not be a mouldy corpse littering its pages.

The problem was - how could I destroy a corpse so completely that no part of it existed to prove that it ever had quickened with life?

A bath of acid? That was invented in the year One.

A furnace? As old as the hills.

Pushing a corpse into a hollow log; shoving it down a mine shaft and blowing tons of earth on to it; taking it to sea in a motor boat and sinking it in a thousand fathoms of water with half a ton of lead - that undoubtedly thrilled our grandfathers. We see so much of it on the screen that we become bored to tears.

On the No. 1 Fence, my headquarters were at the Government Camel station, and every month I stayed three or four days there, one day for every Sunday spent on the track. The man in charge led a life as lonely as mine, and, consequently, we would talk like women over a garden wall, for the sake of hearing a blessed human voice.

And at night, such was our craving for mental excitement, we would run two gramophones and the wireless at the same time in the same room of the comfortable stone-built homestead. To make poker more thrilling, we each secretly marked a pack of cards, and sharpened our wits to prevent the other fellow from cheating too much.

Nemesis

And at this place, I met a young man of about 26, tall, well-built and lithe, good looking, fair-haired and blue-eyed, well spoken, obliging and generous. He called himself Snowy Rowles.

There was about him nothing to suggest the hardened criminal. He rode well enough to grace any rodeo. He drove a motor bicycle with greater skill than ever I have seen on a speedway. He was employed as a stockman on Narndee Station, and his quarters were ten miles west.

As Narndee sheep station almost surrounded the Government property, Rowles would occasionally call and spend a night, when on his way to or from Narndee's outlying mills.

Orders came through that I was to stay at the Camel Station and assist George Gray to break in several camels, and so it came about that I got to know Rowles rather well - or thought I did. And because a man's character is more clearly revealed through his actions than through his words and his facial appearance, here are two illustrations of it.

He arrived one afternoon when Gray and I had become tired of the kangaroo meat and food contained in tins, which is so aptly called tinned dog. On being asked if he had brought any mutton, and receiving a negative answer, he was forcibly requested to go back to his camp and fetch some. With his eyes dancing and a grin on his attractive face, he wheeled the motor bike and set off at a terrific speed. Gray rushed to the wood-heap, and I scoured out the frying-pan. Rowles had been gone half an hour when we saw him careering madly across the stone-littered, rabbit-warrened plain between the house and Dromedary Hill, and presently he mustered into the back yard, still mounted on his machine, a hefty old-man kangaroo.

Another day, he caught George Gray on an open space near the house, and rode at him at fifty miles an hour, to slew the machine off the certain victim in the last yard. For some time, while these charges were made, accompanied by shouts of laughter, George dared not move, but presently opportunity gave him the chance to rush into the kitchen - to be followed by Rowles on the machine, who bailed him up in a corner and filled the kitchen with smoke from a roaring exhaust.

Not the kind of man you would believe was a bag snatcher and a burglar and a gaol-breaker.

Perfect Crime

Before these illustrations of Rowles's character took place, I casually asked Gray if he knew an efficient method of destroying a corpse. I offered him a pound if he could provide me with one both efficient and simple.

"Done. Give us your quid."

"Method first," I said cautiously.

"All right. Supposing I wanted to do you in. I'd take you into the bush, shoot you dead, burn your body, sieve the ashes for all your bones and metal objects such as buttons and boot sprigs. The metal objects I'd throw down several wells, and your bones I would powder to dust in a prospector's dolly pot, and scatter them to the winds. To prevent suspicion regarding the fire, I'd burn a couple of 'roos on the same site."

Having no cash save the pennies with which we played poker, I wrote him an I.O.U, Gray's method was perfect. My problem was solved.

Exactly so - but it produced a second problem, the solution of which was a thousand times more difficult.

Were I to commit a fiction murder and destroy a body according to this method, how was I going to make my murderer commit one mistake; leave one clue for Bony to find and on which to build up his case? As one discerning critic of the resultant novel wrote: "It was the irresistible projectile striking the immovable object, the perfect murder investigated by what must be the perfect detective, and as no human being can possibly be perfect, Upfield had to tamper with the projectile."

But how? Were a man to do such and such and such, where could he make a fatal mistake? I offered Gray another pound if he could solve this second problem which defied me. He was trying hard to do so one day, when, hat-less and unshaven and carrying a rifle, and riding a hack, he met Snowy Rowles on his motor bike. And without any greeting, he said:

"Hey, Snow! If I was to shoot you stone dead this minute, burn your body, dolly-pot your bones, and throw your boot sprigs down a well, how would I get caught?" Rowles, thinking that the bush had at long last "got" Gray, muttering something about being in a hurry, rode away on a zig-zag course, expecting to feel a bullet in his back; and not till several hours later did George Gray discover and tell the joke against himself.

The One Clue

Neither Gray nor Rowles, nor the other fence men solved for me this second problem. I put it to a small gathering of "intellectuals" in Perth without success, and finally I gave it up as being insoluble. And then, months later, when again on the track and I was looking down the shaft camel's roaring throat, the solution flashed into my mind.

I saw how I could provide a clue without detracting an iota from Gray's method. Bony should find that one clue, which should establish both that a man had been killed and who had killed him.

There is no greater mental ecstasy than that experienced when creating a story and its character. No physical sensation can be compared to it.

I went to the Camel Station as manager, Gray leaving, and there I set to work on a novel more cosily written than any, every piece of the jig-saw puzzle falling easily into place.

There came one evening to take dinner with me, and afterwards to depart southward, a grizzled ex-sailor of admirable disposition, one named James Ryan. He was a station contractor, owning his own truck and plant, and he worked on Narndee Station. He promised to return in ten days and bring with him my supplies and mail.

He had been gone ten days when Rowles came, stayed a night, said that Ryan intended to go to the far north west when he came back, and that he, Rowles, was to go with him.

Rowles went south in an old car to meet Ryan, broke down, and was picked up by the returning Ryan. Ryan brought with him a young man as mate named George Lloyd, who said he had recently arrived from Adelaide. That night the three stayed with me, and they set off for Ryan's camp early the next morning, It was the last I saw of either Ryan or Lloyd. They were splendid fellows. Lloyd played a new accordion, accompanying Ryan who had a splendid voice.

A week after they left me, I heard in a roundabout way that they had left Narndee for the north-west. It was no business of mine what they did, for in the bush lands men arrive from nowhere, stay a little while, and depart for nowhere.

A handsome, laughing, gay cavalier had prepared my mind, as well as other minds, to accent the fact of his possession of Ryan's truck as perfectly normal. For him the future hid a disgraceful death; for many of us it hid months of worry. Men may evolve the perfect crime, but there never can be the perfect murderer to commit it or the perfect detective to investigate it, because it is impossible for any man to possess the perfect mind.

"Snowy" Rowles with Ryan's ute, photographed by Arthur Upfield.

11

The Murchison Bones Murder Case

Rowles's Lie

With one of the boundary riders on the Number One Fence, Western Australia, on Christmas Eve I went to the town of Youanmi, where the mine has long been abandoned and all but half a dozen houses and the hotel long since disappeared. It had been early in December when it was thought that Ryan and Lloyd with Rowles, had departed for the North-West, and here on the verandah of the hotel stood Snowy Rowles.

"Hello! Thought you were gone to the North-West with Ryan," I said.

"We got as far as the Mount Magnet pub," Rowles explained easily. "You know what Ryan is in a pub, I borrowed his truck to come over to spend Christmas here. Seeing a girl."

"'Ware skirt, Snowy! Come and have a snifter."

That was a perfectly logical explanation for Rowles to make. Ryan was one of those unfortunates who would stay at an hotel until he was broke or nearly so, and we could picture him mellowed by John Barleycorn and carelessly loaning his truck to a young man who wanted to see his girl. Yet Ryan and Lloyd never were at Mount Magnet.

In the middle of January I left the Camel Station on annual leave, and while in Perth a bush fire destroyed several miles of the fence. When this damage had been repaired, I went back to my old section because at the Camel Station one lived at one place, and on the fence one moved camp every day. I have got to the stage that to in one place more than three months is just plain hell.

A full year went by. I completed *The Sands of Windee,* and in due course received and returned the proofs. I planned an abduction story down to the smallest detail; the story of a visiting princess being taken off the trans train at Cook on the Nullabor Plain, and held to ransom in underground caves near Eucla. Of course, I knew the country and its conditions, but when I laid this plan before a senior police officer, he passed it as being more than feasible.

Yes, a whole year went by in blissful ignorance of what had happened to Ryan and Lloyd. As I have stated, they disappeared, ostensibly leaving the district, in December, 1929, and no one thought to inquire for them. Both belonged to the great travelling public of the interior. Five months after they went - in May, 1930, a New Zealander named Carron was paid off from a station with a cheque for £27. He was seen to drive away with Snowy Rowles, who then was in possession of Ryan's truck for which he had paid £70, so he said.

Suspicion Grows

This year, 1930, witnessed the full blast of the depression and Government retrenchment. Half the fence staff was sacked, and my section was altered to extend one hundred miles north and south of the railway line, with my headquarters at a small wheat town named Burracoppin. Hence I lost touch with the Camel Station.

In the late summer of 1931, the Fence Inspector brought the news that Carron was missing, and that Rowles had cashed his station cheque to buy a case of beer. Relatives in New Zealand, as well as the growing suspicions of his friend on the Murchison, had started police inquiries.

"Looks as though Snowy and Carron were having a quiet tiddly in their camp, and that a row arose in which Carron got killed," was the inspector's opinion. I agreed with him, saying:

"A man is apt to kill another in a drunken brawl any time. Can't they find Carron?"

"No, they are searching the breakaways and looking for old fire sites. They got a plan of all the back tracks from me this trip. Snowy was a fool not to have owned up right away."

"Perhaps he put that book plot of yours into practice," a man with the inspector cut in. "If he did, he'll get away with it."

"They don't get away with that sort of thing in real life, though," the inspector said dryly.

A month passed when the inspector came along again. I read his serious news in his face.

"Ryan and Lloyd are missing now," he said. "No one has seen them since they left the Camel Station with Rowles when you were there."

My brain became cloudy, lethargic, as though unable to function at the imminent stroke of some dreadful calamity. I remember seeing nothing but the inspector's lips, when he went on: "When the police found that Carron was last seen in the company of Rowles, they wanted to know all about him, where he was, what he did. When they heard that he was a fox trapper and general stockman, and was in possession of a good truck, they wanted to know of whom he had bought the truck. That led them to look for Ryan, and they can't find him or Lloyd."

"Never Saw Them"

"But Ryan and Lloyd went to Mount Magnet. They were there when Snowy borrowed the truck and came to Youanmi that Christmas. They must remember them at Mount Magnet," I objected.

They know nothing about them at Mount Magnet. Never saw them. No one has seen them since they left the Camel Station," the inspector said emphatically. "Now, look here. The police on the job know all about you, and all about that book plot. You take my advice and send in a statement."

"If they want a statement from me let them come and get it. I'm not going to be dragged into a thing like that if I can help it."

"Whether you like it or not, you will be dragged into it. If you don't make a statement, later on you will be asked why you didn't. The fact of Carron's disappearance is public property. You can't plead ignorance, even on this fence."

Here was mental food for a lonely man with a vengeance. What so worried me was not two facts separated, but two facts in conjunction. I had made known a perfect murder plot, and I had been the last person to see Ryan and Lloyd other than Rowles. If Rowles was to swear that I was his accomplice, I would be well in the soup, because during that life of solitude at the Camel Station I could not call on a living soul to back me.

Arrived at the Fence Headquarters at Burracoppin, the Inspector asked if I had written the statement. I had not. I was horrified by the prospect of being drawn into such an affair. When on my way to the boarding house that evening to dinner, the publican waylaid me to urge with the inspector's arguments that I make a voluntary statement, and because I was sensible enough to know that these two men rendered advice in a spirit of friendship, I sent down a typed statement, the like of which never appeared in the most fantastic fiction.

I expected one of any half-dozen results, but not the prolonged silence. The statement was not even acknowledged. From the Murchison nothing came out. The regularly-visiting inspector could learn nothing. An official fog of secrecy fell over all that vast district. When the police went to question Rowles they recognised in him a man whose name was not Rowles, a man who was wanted for breaking gaol where he was waiting on a burglary charge. They arrested him for breaking gaol; later he was tried for burglary and received three years. The police had three years to conduct their investigations of the disappearance of those three men. The affair became likened to the slowly-working mills of God.

That Rowles might have killed Carron, yes. That then he might foolishly have attempted to destroy the body, yes. But that he was a burglar and had served a term of imprisonment for bag snatching in Perth was utterly incredible to us who knew the man on the Murchison. For the two years that we knew him he had not stolen so much as a piece of washing soap. When at the Camel Station, more than once I had returned from a day among the stock to find him repairing his motor with the Government's tools. The whole house was open. He could have gone through my personal belongings and stolen one or more of my pay cheques, and I would never have known he had been there.

It is unnecessary to follow the official case too closely. Rowles had failed to sift thoroughly the ashes of several fires at a place known as the 183-mile. In the ashes of those year-old fires were found human bones, natural and false teeth which in number and composition coincided with those known to be in Carron's mouth; Mrs Carron's wedding ring which Carron always wore; a splash of lead equal in weight to a .32 rifle bullet; and masses of kangaroo bones. At Ryan's camp they found eight fire sites in which were found belt Buckles and boot sprigs and buttons; unidentifiable bones and kangaroo bones; and the bones of Lloyd's brand new accordion which most certainly he never would have burned.

Burning Rubbish

After all, I was not the last person to see those two men in Rowles company. A prospector saw them in Ryan's camp the evening of the day they left me. When, a few days after that, the owner of Narndee Station visited the camp, he found Rowles cooking, and actually had his lunch with Rowles. Rowles said that Ryan and Lloyd ware away working, and he explained a large fire in the vicinity of the camp by saying that he was burning a lot of useless camp rubbish.

The Sands of Windee was published in London, and was selected as the book of the month by the Crime Book Society. The leading literary journals such as *The Times Literary Supplement*, *The London Bookman*, and the *Oxford Times* gave it excellent notices, agreeing that it was a good novel beside being a good detective story.

Time went on, as it must. I went to live in Perth. One bookseller told me that the Western Australian Crown Prosecutor had bought a copy of the book; another that four detectives walked into his shop and each bought a copy. Still no interview with me. I felt much as a fly must do when entangled in the web of a spider who is in no hurry to begin.

But the arm of the law had to reach me.

"I am Detective-Sergeant Manning," said a military looking man, whose grey eyes had the trick of opening to the size of saucers. And then, smiling with genuine amusement, he added: "I've come along to have a chat about *The Sands of Windee*."

No bluff, no trickery, no Third Degree methods; Manning is too clever to use such stupid artifices. A born bushman, he is pre-eminent in bush crimes. He had summed me up long before he set his gaze at me, and I found it much easier to explain things to him than when later I had to explain things to city people.

"Fatal Flaw"

The trial lasted eight days. It was remarkable how Manning's investigations so closely followed the investigation conducted by Bony in the book.

We are coming to understand a little the problem of dual personality so ably "romanticised" by Stevenson in his Jekyll-Hyde story, but we cannot apply the personality of Mr Hyde to Snowy Rowles. Hyde murdered for the sheer lust to kill; Rowles murdered for gain. But, with Mr Hyde, Rowles revealed consummate cunning in successfully keeping hidden the personality which thought murder before it planned murder. It was a personality which existed in the same body with one of exceeding attraction to men as well as to women.

Most men who facilely attract women are not liked by men, but Rowles was. He had all the manly virtues; courage, outstanding ability with horses, an excellent shot, a fine bushman. He possessed a high sense of humor, and his nature was generous. Of the 50 odd witnesses against him, there was not one who did not earnestly desire that he would be proved innocent. Their hearts wanted to believe that which their brains refused to accept and had he been proved innocent there is no doubt that his return to the Murchison would have been in the nature of a triumph.

The judge's summing up was terrible. Calm, passionless, that icy cold voice of Justice was the most dreadful thing I have heard.

"You fool, Rowles! You fool to think you could get away with it. Vanity was your besetting sin and your final destruction. You conceived yourself to be the perfect murderer when all men will ever be imperfect. You followed the plot of the *Sands of Windee* which, after all, contains one fatal flaw which you blindly put into practice. In real life, there never has been and never will be the perfect murder."

"Snowy" Rowles.

12

The Irresistible Call Of The Wild

Mary's Influence

MARY - her surname does not matter - was and is of those women known by every fortunate man, no matter what his station in lite, no matter what kind of life he has led. This particular Mary was tall, straight and gaunt. I saw pictures of her dressed in the fashions of long ago. and in them she was beautiful. When I first knew her. she was tall and gaunt.

Her husband was killed by bolting buggy horses, and he left her with a small station and two little children. Did she rush home to mother? She did not. She carried on, nature working her face with the plastic surgery of hard labor into those fixed lines of gauntness. But she was able to make her son a doctor and her daughter second edition of what once she was. And what once she was a man glimpsed when he looked into her grey eyes and felt the urge to wind his fingers among the tresses of her snow-white hair.

I blame Mary for making me incapable of drawing a wicked woman character in my novels. Try hard as I may, I never can muster sufficient hate and loathing to draw a proper vlllainness! Memory of Mary always intrudes. The greatest want that your young immigrant experiences is the influence of a good woman, and he sustains that want when at the most impressionable age of his life. Which is why the Big Brother movement should be maintained and extended at all personal cost when the stream of immigration begins again to flow.

I had been in Australia three years when I met Mary. I worked and saved money - to spend recklessly in town or city, I lived hard both ways, and Mary tried to show me that I was getting nowhere, and would never get anywhere, along the path I was treading. When I told her of my lost dreams of a farm and a home; when I confessed to my backbone-lessness, and pictured two young people fooled so superbly by vivid immigration literature, she came to understand how it was I lived only for the day; how it was I had no ambition but to keep moving on like Jules Verne's Captain Hatteras.

In The City

I could myself see that this constant rushing about; this demanding my cheque and walking hundreds of miles before accepting the next job, certainly would not take me anywhere worthwhile, and on Mary's advice, I went to Sydney with about £40, determined to get a city job, stick to it, and become a captain of industry.

Whereas, on a former visit I had spent £198 in three weeks, this time I rigidly kept expenditure down to £4 a week. Discovering no possible hope of taking up my profession, I went to work as a warehouse clerk, and occupied my leisure with writing a novel which no publisher could be expected to accept, and paragraphs which *The Bulletin* failed to find of literary merit.

But - it was of no use. A gardener burning gum leaves in the park, Sunday visits to the Zoo to see the camels, the horse bell summoning us to meals at the boarding house, in combination were too strong for me. I had tasted freedom: I craved and craved for more. The boss caught me reading Lawson's collected verse under the title of *While the Billy Boils*, and began to roar. I told him with great pleasure to keep the job, walked out, and caught the next train to Burke.

From a drover's camp beside the Diamantina, I wrote to Mary and admitted my lack of staying power. I sent her the MS of the novel, and she replied in a ten-page letter urging me to save my money and stick to writing. Later on she wrote again to say that she had burned the MS and advised me to surrender all honors to the Russians who long had raised the lurid sex novel to a fine art.

Came the war. I wrote a war book in 1916; was advised to submit it to a Sydney daily, as all war stuff was cornered by writers who foretold the end of the war to fall on the next day. I was but a common digger, and could not see the war ending the next day. In time, I enquired of the post office about the MS and was curtly informed that it had been "sunk by enemy action." The Germans evidently did not like the adventures of a bachelor in Cairo.

One-Spur Dick

After the war, I wrote short stories for the *Novel Magazine*, and 300-word articles for the *Daily Mail*. I became confidential secretary to the head of a big ordnance depot in the south of England - but I still heard the tinkle of horse bells; could still smell the scent of burning gum leaves; could still see the track winding across the limitless salt-bush plains.

Returning to Australia, I went bush with the eagerness of a man going to his bride. During the long absence I had suffered, joyed, loved and sorrowed, but I had not lived. I knew I had not lived.

I found One-Spur Dick living in a bag humpy, on the river bank near Wilcannia. He was going blind. I was broke but happy. He stoked the fire as he used once to do, and I read to him paper-backed novels until I could read no longer, and he then recounted the stories in detail which I had read to him 10 years previously.

Strike-a-Light George had died at Bullecourt. I bet he growsed that last morning about the tucker, and I bet that he died game. In 1924 I met Jake the Hangman, and he shortened my drop by 11 inches, sorrowing at my lost weight. I never saw Pompey George again, but I heard he rose to be a major in the Camel Corps Transport in Egypt.

The only person of the many I had known before the war, who did not welcome me back to the bush was Mary. Mary cried, which was no welcome. Mary fed me with fresh scones and cream and jam, which was better than crying. Then she lectured me, which was not so nice. I remember her lecture because of its downright commonsense.

"A Waster"

"This is what you have done," she said in tones both soft and kind, but which hurt much more than had she screamed at me. "You have thrown away a profession. You have thrown away chance after chance. You are no better off today than you were 16 years ago. In fact, you are worse off, because you are 16 years older. You are nothing but a waster; a failure, and if you are not careful you will throw away the one talent you have left. As you are so mad about the bush, why don't you tell people outside the bush all about it? To my knowledge you have written seven worthless books. Write about the bush: write about the bush people; write about me. If you like."

So it was that I came to see I could still cling to the real Australia, and regain ambition to make something of life.

Mary was my Big, Big Sister. Seventy-two she will be this year, and still running her station. Just before writing this article on my verandah watching the giant shadow of Mount Dandenong creep across the valley to Little Joe and Mount Donna Buang, I watched the shadow reach Warburton and engulf it, watched it creep up the timbered slopes of Mount Donna Buang. Above that mountain all day long had hung a peg cloud which appeared undecided whether to evaporate or turn into an active water-dog.

The valley sank deeper and deep; into the blue shadow. Donna Buang shed its warm, purple cloak, and rayed over itself the bed quilt of deep blue night. Above it, seeming to be beyond it, the cloud became a leaping flame, though the very world around Neeam South was burning as Hell is alleged to be.

Bush University

And like this day which is past, life is so short and there is yet so much to see and to do. With the passage of the years, each year slips by the faster. I never have done any good for myself or for anyone else, but I have learned the art of living in a hard school. It was no university education, and the syllabus does not contain the study of dead languages and dead literature. I am less interested in the travels of Ulysses than in the travels of Jake the Hangman, and much less interested in Latin than in the more modern language easily spoken by One-Spur Dick to his mules and bullocks.

Dick's language could shift ten tons across hundreds of miles of virgin country. What classical language could do that? And again, what were the achievements of Ulysses - a fool who did not know a good poker hand when he had it - compared with the achievement of Mary, aye, and of the hundreds of other Marys and Johns whose faith in the real Australia never waned, whose love for this land remained ever true? Their great university of the will has been my university. I thank that English doctor who caused a fool to be sent out here, and I thank God that I figuratively kicked my profession in the seat of its pants. A fine house, a beautiful car, a million or two in the bank or less than nothing when weighed in the scales against content with little things and life in the world of the One-Spur Dicks, and Marys, and Irish Muldoons.

I thank God that the living personality of the bush has got its fingers dug into the roots of my soul.

13

The Blankets That Wouldn't "Stay Put"

There used to be a hut in the vicinity of a well, west of Wilcannia, on the Darling, that most certainly seemed to be haunted. Somewhere back in its history, a camel rider hurried to the place to gain shelter from a thunderstorm, and just as he was alighting from his mount a flash of lightning killed both man and animal.

Afterwards several men swore that they had seen the ghost of a man on the back of the ghost of a camel arrive, and halt near the well. The human ghost then walked swiftly to the hut and disappeared within it!

Twelve years after the tragedy I reached the place just before night fell one evening in June, when the ground was soggy with water and the south wind blew with icy temperature across a cloudless sky. Ghost or no ghost, I determined to camp for the night in that hut.

Beside the well I "hooshed" down the three camels, and unloaded them. They hated to kneel there, and only after leading them away some two hundred yards was I able to hobble them. Then, when the noselines had been removed, they incontinently bolted, their hobbled fore-legs making great lunging strides. Without doubt, they were badly frightened by the locality.

An excellent beginning!

Having carried the gear into the hut, I made a fire and placed the filled billy over the flame, and then gathered a supply of wood from the encircling scrub, as the full moon rose whitely from the eastern timber. Half an hour later the iron chimney showed blotches of red heat, and the family was dining on damper, cold mutton chops, and milkless, but well sugared, tea.

There I sat on the tucker box, pleasurably warmed by the fire, with Hool-em-up on one side and Tum-tum, the cat on the other. Both the cat and the dog should have been enjoying the shelter and the warmth, for the dog had run at least 200 miles that day, and the cat had ridden for nearly ten hours in her especial pack-bag. But they were obviously uneasy, like the camels, who were frightened by their surroundings.

The south wind whistled and moaned, whispered and shrieked.

When the cooking damper was rising in its bed of ashes. I made up my bunk so that I could read by the firelight, as the supply of fat was becoming short; and when the damper had been removed from the ashes and was cooling on its edge. I lay on the bunk reading a particularly thrilling thriller.

I was just at that part of the book where the madman was on the point of cutting the heroine's throat when the hut rocked beneath a terrific blow. In a split second I was on my feet facing the door, Hool-em-up was crouched hard against my legs, hackles stiff with fright, and Tum-tum was standing on stiffened legs on one of the cross beams supporting the roof. From outside came a low hissing noise. A dull thud came from beyond the door.

Then with dreadful slowness the door began to open inwards.

I looked for a window through which to escape. There was none. The only egress was through the slowly opening door beyond which - ! With a howl Hool-em-up dashed forward. He howled again as he disappeared through the doorway. He yelped as he fled to the scrub. The cat hissed and spat. No longer was it possible for me to remain inactive.

With a flaming wood billet from the fire held aloft, I charged wildly as the dog had clone, the door by this time being wide open. Beyond it the well and the dark scrub lay revealed in the brilliant moonlight. 1 leaped outside, the torch presented like a sword. I trod on something which yielded and gave a moan of anguish.

A hundred yards separated me from the haunted hut when I stopped at last and returned, pride spurring my deadened feet. I saw nothing, could hear nothing but the wind. But outside the door lay the body of a heavy black duck which, mistaking the iron roof, reflecting the moonlight, for water, had crashed to its death on it! Hool-em-up did not appear until morning, and the three camels were then as far away as they could get - in a paddock corner nine miles distant.

But, all the same, I never camped at that hut again.

Then there was the Haunted Fence - and here originality is claimed for the locality of a haunting,

With two dogs and a galah I was camped beside a dog-proof fence. At that moment before falling to sleep, when the mind is in its most receptive state, the dogs began to whimper, and, on sitting up to look in the direction they indicated, I saw, approaching along the fence, a great white Thing, rising and sinking alternately.

In the presence of a ghost inactivity spells retreat.

The Thing was now quite close. The dogs were emphatically scared. So was I, but I managed to point the shot gun and press both triggers at the same moment. From the fence something white dashed away - and at the foot of the fence something white lay still.

Poor thing! It was only a goat, which had been engaged in friendly argument with another goat on the other side of the fence. It was quite a young goat, and we profited by the fright!

And now having broached the subject of ghosts in an easy, anecdotal fashion, the subject will be treated with more respect; for, after all, there may be real ghosts which are not the creation of imagination or of indigestion, ghosts whose presence a man can feel and animals can see. Consequently the following experience can be supplied with no adequate explanation.

At the close of a brilliant day in late August I selected a patch of clean sandy ground, beside a billabong off the Warrego, on which to camp for the night. I was alone, my dog having picked up a poison bait four days previously. After supper, having cooked a damper and some meat for the morrow, I gathered my bushman's mattress composed of leaves, laid upon it a strip of waterproof sheeting and one blanket, and dropped off to sleep with three blankets over me and a roaring, leaping fire beside me.

I woke to find that the fire had subsided into a mound of red coals, and that the three blankets lay in a heap about a yard from my feet. Puzzled to account for this, and too sleepy to bother about it, I replenished the fire, re-arranged the blankets, and slept again. And again I awoke to find myself very cold, the fire low, and my blankets in a pile about a yard beyond my feet.

It was then just after two o'clock, the night being dark and silent. For two hours I sat before a leaping fire and pondered over this strange series of incidents. At length, wearied by unanswerable questions, I composed myself for the third time and slept.

And for the third time did I awake to feel the cold of death, and to find the blankets in that singular pile beyond my feet. In a kind of numbed frenzy I gathered wood and threw it on the lire until a tall column of flame was shooting skywards and driving back the encroaching shadows. Without real justification I was mastered by fear - fear which directed my feet to carry my body at top speed through the blanketed darkness; fear braked only by the knowledge that surrender to panic would result in possible fatal injury through collision against a tree, or a fall into a cliff-sided billabong. And until day broke I walked round and round the fire, feeling that something was watching me, wrestling with the demon which rode me.

For two hours I searched diligently for tracks in the vicinity of the camp, to find none of man or beast or bird save my own. I could understand a man throwing his blankets to one side or the other; I could understand getting up and tossing the blankets into a pile in that unlikely position, and returning to bed without remembering the act. But I could not understand the exact triplication of those acts. There was, and is, no explanation!

From an old aboriginal I learned afterwards that on that camp site a lubra and her paramour had been killed by the woman's tribal owner. Was it she who had teased me that night? Does a ghost have the power to lift blankets?

If so, she most certainly must have enjoyed the spectacle presented by a white man walking round and round his camp fire with every single hair of his head on end.

The minx!

14

Whitewashing a Police Station

The summer had been long and hot, and the autumn rains delayed in coming. For a year almost I had lived at the edge of a great gibber plain in the far north-east of South Australia, the small hut of iron sheets and its wide verandah roof of cane grass being situated above a lone water-hole in the bed of a creek.

At noon every day there came to the creek a flock of fourteen emus, and at sundown there arrived Iky Mo, Eliza, Dad, the Old Man, Ethel and Flo, and Blue and Brown - otherwise a family of eight kangaroos. It is needless to mention the many birds.

The two dogs and the five cats came to tolerate both the emus and the 'roos which arrived with the regularity of sunrise. Over five months their numbers neither increased nor decreased, the country being in fair condition and offering them no hardships.

Then one day in May they failed to appear. The camp at eventide seemed strangely deserted. They came not again, and even when I saw the buck rabbits sitting on the highest points of their burrows, I did not guess the reason for their desertion; no, not even when I noticed how the rabbits were spiritedly twitching their nostrils.

About a fortnight after my friends vanished, there came along a half-caste dog-trapper who told me that down around Broken Hill it had rained about two and a half inches. The south wind had brought northward the smell of rain-soaked earth and the promise of springing green herbage, which proved an irresistible magnet to all things which flew and ran.

Perhaps it was the south wind whispering of cool days and cold nights to come which aroused the migratory instinct within me, for that evening I rang up the manager and asked if the half-caste could take my place immediately.

Thus it came about that with a bank book proving a credit balance of £88 and a station cheque made in my favour for £30, I met Blue Peter, a stocky little man with red hair and blue eyes, and a winning smile. Together, we tramped towards Hergott Springs, each bicycle loaded with a swag and tucker.

For the reason that I liked the sergeant and kissed the sergeant's daughter, I am not going to mention the name of the township this particular police sergeant controlled. He was an unorthodox policeman who, however, knew his job and his people, and efficiently ran a huge district, the capital of which was a two-pub, post office-cum-store, twenty-house town. Beside the police station was erected a one cell lockup.

Arrived in town, Blue Peter went along to the baker, and I had the station cheque transferred to my bank account which was thereby swelled to £118. That was late in the afternoon, and whilst waiting for my companion, I sat on the wooden kerbing on the sidewalk outside the store. Then the sergeant strolled to my side.

He was a jovial looking, white-haired man, with kindly brown eyes and a grim, determined jaw.

"Where you come from?" he asked gruffly.

"Way down from Swanee River," I replied with unwaiverable flippancy.

"Oh! have you! And where are you going?"

"To my Old Grey Home in the West, sergeant."

"Well, well, well! Many a true word spoken in jest. Now you just take a little walk with me."

And before I knew what was what, I was safely lodged in the one-cell prison, the walls of which were washed grey.

On the hard trestle bed I unrolled my swag and made myself

comfortable, for the sergeant told me I would be there all night. Then a trap door in the door proper was slid upwards and a pair of dark-brown solemn eyes regarded me in cool and calm judgement.

"What are you in there for?" asked the sergeant's daughter.

"I'm here because I told the sergeant I was making for My Little Grey Home in the West, and he kindly helped me to my destination."

"Oh! Are you hungry? - I am"

"What is your name?"

"My friends call me Hampshire."

With that the trap door dropped into place.

Half an hour later the Sergeant's daughter brought me tea and bread and butter and jam on a tray. She unbolted the door and walked in with the provender after she had seriously besought and gained my promise not to escape. It turned out that the sergeant's lady and I originated on either side of Portsmouth harbour, and the sergeant's daughter and I discovered mutual interest in the George Hotel, in which is still the bed Lord Nelson occupied during his last night ashore; and talked of his flagship, the Victory, now in dry dock for ever, and the plaque in the high wall above the spot where the gay Duke of Buckingham was assassinated.

She had left with the tray when I heard outside Blue Peter pleading to be locked up with me. He was pleading not with the sergeant, but with the sergeant's daughter, who, without much demur, opened the door to admit him and lock it again upon us both. Having heard of my fate, Blue Peter stored his machine, bought three bottles of beer and a pound of tobacco, and decided to camp with me.

The next morning the sergeant said to him: "What are you doing in here? How did you get in?"

"Well, I was looking for My Little Grey Home in the West, and I reckon I found it last night when your pretty daughter opened the door."

"Well, well, well! Had breakfast yet?"

"Yes, sergeant. Your daughter did not forget to bring it."

The sergeant returned about an hour after that, and hailed us before the "beak." Without visible means of support, was the charge.

"Plead," snapped the "beak."

"Guilty, you honour," replied Blue Peter, without hesitation. "Seven days," announced the Court.

I never regained breath until I was back in the cell, and then began to remonstrate with my fellow prisoner. He said: "What are you worrying about? We've got board and lodgings for a full week. We'll get three good meals a day and a real rest."

The sergeant came in to say: "Now, boys, you play the game and we'll get on all right. I want the station whitewashed. Do a fair thing and you'll find I won't be hard. What about it?"

"A little gentle exercise will do me, sergeant," assented Blue Peter, and, because it was useless to kick against the pricks, I concurred with him.

The Law immediately relaxed its vigilance. Blue Peter and I got to work making up the whitewash, and at noon the sergeant's lady announced lunch. She and the sergeant and the sergeant's daughter and the two prisoners sat at a table in the sergeant's kitchen. The sergeant's lady was about fifty years old, and she and I talked Portsmouth till nearly two o'clock, when the interested policeman suggested work. The sergeant's daughter wanted to mutiny, but received no support.

At five o'clock the sergeant instructed me to purchase from one of the hotels two bottles of beer with the four shillings he gave. The work and the bottles of beer gave to us prisoners an excellent appetite, and, after dinner, whilst the sergeant went hunting for the illusive desperate characters, we sat in his parlour with the sergeant's daughter running the gramophone. When he returned without any desperate characters, he locked up for the night the two he did have.

Three excellent meals and a bottle of beer every day for a week. As Blue Peter said: What more could any man desire? The sergeant was delighted with the newly-whitewashed police station, and contemplated charging us with disorderly behaviour in order to retain our services another week to have the front fence repaired.

Our last night I bought four bottles of beer and the largest box of lollies in the store for the sergeant's daughter, whom I had come to know was madly in love with me. When the sergeant, on the following morning, advised us to get employment, I showed him my bank book in proof that I really did have substantial means of support.

"Goodbye, Hampshire. I wish daddy would lock you up again. Come back soon, so that he can," cried the sergeant's daughter.

Her eyes were very bright, and she wanted to be kissed. She was only twelve.

Arthur Upfield Stories - first publication in 1934

1. Led by a Child, *The Listener*, 6 January 1934, p12.

2. **Going Bush:** My Life Outback Starts, *The Herald*, Melbourne, 12 January 1934, p12; My Life Outback No 1: A Dream and the Sad Awakening, *The Advertiser,* Adelaide, 13 January 1934, p15; Up and Down Australia No 1: Going Bush," *The West Australian*, Perth, 26 January 1934, p3.

3. Poison! *The Herald*, Melbourne, 13 January 1934, p33.

4. **One-Spur Dick:** My Life Outback No 2: One Spur Dick, *The Herald*, Melbourne, 13 January 1934, p24; My Life Outback No 2: On the Road with a Mule Team, *The Advertiser,* Adelaide, 20 January 1934, p20; Up and Down Australia No 2: Mule Driver's Offsider, *The West Australian,* Perth, 2 February 1934, p16.

5. **Opal Gouging:** My Life Outback No 3: Opal Gouging with Big Jack - and his Cat, *The Herald,* Melbourne, 15 January 1934, p19; My Life Outback No 3: Opal ! Empress of Precious Stones, *The Advertiser*, Adelaide, 27 January 1934, p9; Up and Down Australia No 3: Opal, Empress of Stones, *The West Australian*, Perth, 7 February 1934, p18.

6. **Camels and a Fence:** My Life Outback No 4: Dire Tale of Goanna and Two Camels, *The Herald*, Melbourne, 16 January 1934, p17; My Life Outback No 4: The Dog, a Goanna and Two Camels, *The Advertiser,* Adelaide, 3 February 1934,

7. **Tramping by the Darling**: My Life Outback No 5: On the Tramp by the Darling, *The Herald*, Melbourne, 17 January 1934, p16; My Life Outback No 5: Tramping by the Darling, *The Advertiser*, Adelaide, 10 February 1934, p11; Up and Down Australia No 5: Tramping by the Darling, *The West Australian*, Perth, 10 February 1934, p14.

8. **Fighting the Thirst-mad Mob** My Life Outback No 6: Fighting the Thirst-mad Mob, *The Herald*, Melbourne, 18 January 1934, p31; Up and Down Australia No 6: Wells and Water Troughs, *The West Australian*, Perth, 12 February 1934, p13; My Life Outback No 6: Frenzied Rush to Drink, *The Advertiser,* Adelaide, 17 February 1934, p11.

9. **When Crabby Tom Ran Amok**: My Life Outback No 7: When Crabby Tom Ran Amok, *The Herald*, Melbourne, 19 January 1934, p20; Up and Down Australia No 7: Cooks and their Habits, *The West Australian*, Perth, 13 February 1934, p18; My Life Outback No 7: Crabby Tom and his DTs, *The Advertiser*, 24 February 1934.

10. **Sand Storm Terror in Sturt's Country**: My Life Outback No 8: Sand-storm Terror in Sturt's Country, *The Herald*, Melbourne, 20 January 1934, p32; Up and Down Australia No 8: A Dog-proof Fence Job, *The West Australian*, Perth, 14 February 1934, p6; My Life Outback No 8: Guarding a Border Fence, *The Advertiser*, Adelaide, 3 March 1934, p9.

11. **Mad Fever of the Skin Game**: My Life Outback No 9: Mad Fever of the Skin Game, *The Herald*, Melbourne, 22 January 1934, p10; Up and Down Australia No 9: Fur Fever, *The West Australian*, Perth, 17 February 1934, p5; My Life Outback No 9: Fever of the Skin Game, *The Advertiser*, Adelaide, 10 March 1934, p9.

12."**Snowy" Rowles, Gay Daredevil**: My Outback Life No 10: "Snowy" Rowles, Gay Daredevil, *The Herald,* Melbourne, 23 January 1934; A Nearly Perfect Crime: Solving the Murchison Bones Case, *The Advertiser*, Adelaide, 24 March 1934, p 11.

13: **The Murchison Bones Murder Case**: My Outback Life No. 11: The Murchison Bones Murder Case, *The Herald,* Melbourne, 24 January 1934; also published as Plot for a Murder Mystery: Planning a Perfect Crime: *Adelaide Advertiser*, 17 March 1934

14. **The Irresistable Call of the Wild:** My Life Outback No 12: The Irresistible Call of the Wild, *The Herald*, Melbourne, 25 January 1934, p22; Up and Down Australia No 12: Call of the Wild, *The West Australian*, Perth, 22 February 1934, p18.

15. The Melody Hut, *The Herald*, Melbourne, 3 March 1934; The Real Australia (3): The Musical Hut, *The West Australian*, Perth, 12 March 1934, p16; The Real Australia, *The Adelaide Chronicle*, 6 June 1935, p 47.

16. The Gentle Grafter: The Real Australia (2): The Gentle Grafter, *The West Australian*, Perth, 6 March 1934, p20.

17. **The Blankets That Wouldn't 'Stay Put'**: Some Outback Ghosts: The Blankets That Wouldn't "Stay Put, *The Herald*, Melbourne, 7 July 1934, p33.

18. Fun for the Afternoon: A Tale of an Intelligent Bull in the Outback, *The Herald,* Melbourne, 28 July 1934, p33.

19. My Old Pal, Buller, *The Herald*, Melbourne, 10 March 1934, p33; The Real Australia (8): A Scorpion and Two Camels, *The West Australian, Perth,* 28 March 1934, p20.

20. The Sheep They Couldn't Kill, *The Herald*, Melbourne, 17 March 1934, p14; The Real Australia (5): Lombroso and a Ration Sheep, *The West Australian*, Perth, 21 March 1934, p13.

21. A Cure for Snakebite: The Real Australia (4): The Antidote, *The West Australian*, Perth, 19 March 1934, p18; A Cure for Snakebite, *The Herald*, Melbourne, 24 March 1934, p32; The Real Australia, *The Adelaide Chronicle*, 6 June 1935, p47.

22. **Whitewashing a Police Station**: The Real Australia (6): Whitewashing a Police Station, *The West Australian,* Perth, 23 March 1934, p26; Whitewashing a Police Station, *The Herald,* Melbourne, 7 April 1934, p32.

23. Waiting for Rain: The Real Australia (7): Trials of a Squatter, *The West Australian*, Perth, 26 March 1934, p18; The Real Australia: How They Waited for the Rain: The Courage of One Woman, *The Herald,* Melbourne, 31 March 1934, p15

24. The River Pirate: The Real Australia (9): The River Pirate, *The West Australian,* Perth, 2 April 1934, p4; The Pirate of the Darling, *The Herald,* Melbourne, 14 April 1934, p33.

25. The Strike Leader: The Real Australia (10): The Strike Leader, *The West Australian*, Perth, 3 April 1934, p14.

26. Ever Backwards: The Real Australia (11): Ever Backwards, *The West Australian,* Perth, 7 April 1934, p20.

27. Chasing the Rainbow: The Real Australia (12): Chasing the Rainbow, *The West Australian,* Perth, 16 April 1934, p12.

28. One Digger's War No 1: How the Boys Went into Camp, *The Herald,* Melbourne, 19 April 1934, p22.

29. One Digger's War No 2: All Aboard - and Columbo Invaded, *The Herald,* Melbourne, 20 April 1934, p22.

30. One Digger's War: Ducks for Christmas Dinner, *The Herald,* Melbourne, 21 April 1934, p32.

31. One Digger's War No 4: Laughter and Death at Gallipoli, *The Herald,* Melbourne, 23 April 1934, p17.

32. One Digger's War No 5: When the Germans Nearly Won, *The Herald,* Melbourne, 24 April 1934, p20.

33. When Influenza Comes to Stay: Vagaries of a Germ in Flanders Mud and Outback, *The Herald*, Melbourne, 28 May 1934, p6; *The Advertiser,* 26 May 1934; Why This Influenza? *The West Australian,* 23 June 1934, p5; Please Banish Influenza, *The Adelaide Chronicle*, 31 May 1934.

34. My Money on the Rain: A Memory of Outback Days, *The Herald,* Melbourne, 23 June 1934, p32; An Outback Marriage - and its Chains: The Dream That Did Not Come True, *The Herald*, Melbourne, 4 August 1934, p33.

35. Mice and Men, *The Bulletin*, Sydney, 4 July 1934, p48.

36. Kissing the Capitalists, *The Bulletin*, Sydney, 8 August 1934, p48-49.

37. Giving to Get: A Centenary Moral, *The Herald,* Melbourne, 18 August 1934, p6.

38. Why Markham Bought a Radio Set, *The Listener-In*, 18 August 1934, pp16-17.

39. The Man Who Laughed Last: Old Man Angus and the Kangaroo Steak! *The Herald,* Melbourne, 25 August 1934, p33.

40. Pimple's Elixir, *The Bulletin*, Sydney, 12 September 1934,p 49-50.

41. The Outback Changes: What Mechanised Age Has Done, *The Herald*, Melbourne, 29 September 1934, p6.

42. Chefs of the Outback: The Real Test of Good Cooking, *The Herald,* Melbourne, 22 December 1934, p29.

43. George's Accommodating Brother, *The Bulletin*, Sydney, 26 December 1934, pp40 - 41.

The Murchison Murders, The Midget Masterpiece Publishing Company, Sydney.

Other Titles by Arthur W. Upfield and published by ETT Imprint:

Upfield's own drawing of Bony

Bony Novels by Upfield:

www.ingramcontent.com/pod-product-compliance
Lightning Source LLC
Chambersburg PA
CBHW041605240626
47164CB00008B/185